"Hey guys," Jen called as she sidled up to the group. "So, you psyched, Dawson?"

"About *what*?" Dawson asked.

Pacey shook his head and sighed. "You really should consider reading the morning newspaper, Dawson. It told all."

They walked over to the bulletin board, and Dawson read the flyer posted there.

Bick Productions will be shooting the new teen horror movie, *Dripping Red* in Capeside beginning next week. Seeking gofers, extras, assistants of various types. Interviews on Tuesday at the Capeside Inn 3 P.M. to 8 P.M. Bring resume, photo, all pertinent information.

"What is it, a student film?" Dawson asked. "I mean, what's the big deal about some college thing that—"

"I hate to burst your self-involved artistic bubble, Dawson," Jen said, "but it's a feature film. As in major motion picture."

"Really." Dawson scratched his chin. "So . . . this could be something of an opportunity."

Don't miss any of these
DAWSON'S CREEK™ books
featuring your favorite characters!

Dawson's Creek™ The Beginning of Everything Else
*A novelization based on the hit television show
produced by Columbia TriStar Television*

• Seven new, original stories featuring your favorite
characters from **Dawson's Creek**™, the hit television
show.

LONG HOT SUMMER
CALM BEFORE THE STORM
SHIFTING INTO OVERDRIVE
MAJOR MELTDOWN
TROUBLE IN PARADISE
TOO HOT TO HANDLE
DON'T SCREAM

And don't miss:

• **Dawson's Creek**™ The Official Scrapbook
• **Dawson's Creek**™ The Official Postcard Book

Available now from Pocket Books.

Check wherever books are available.

Visit Pocket Books on the World Wide Web
http://www.SimonSays.com

Visit the Sony website at
http://www.dawsonscreek.com

For orders other than by individual consumers, Pocket Books
grants a discount on the purchase of **10 or more** copies of
single titles for special markets or premium use. For further
details, please write to the Vice President of Special Markets,
Pocket Books, 1230 Avenue of the Americas, 9th Floor,
New York, NY 10020-1586.

For information on how individual consumers can place
orders, please write to Mail Order Department, Simon &
Schuster Inc., 100 Front Street, Riverside, NJ 08075.

Dawson's Creek™
Don't Scream

Based on the television series "Dawson's Creek"™
created by **Kevin Williamson**

Written by **C. J. Anders**

POCKET PULSE
New York London Toronto Sydney Singapore

An *Original* Publication of POCKET BOOKS

 POCKET PULSE, published by
POCKET BOOKS, a division of Simon & Schuster Inc.
1230 Avenue of the Americas, New York, NY 10020

ISBN: 0-671-03529-0

First Pocket Pulse printing November 1999

10 9 8 7 6 5 4 3 2 1

For Mike

Don't Scream

Chapter 1

"So I'm just curious, Dawson," Pacey Witter began, lolling against the locker next to Dawson's, as Dawson spun his combination lock. "What do you love more, film or Joey?"

Dawson shot him a bemused look. "What kind of question is that?" He pulled his locker open.

"The kind that will distract me from the mind-numbing hell that is Capeside High School minus Andie McPhee at my side," Pacey replied. "Also, it's rather provocative and intriguing."

"I was thinking more along the lines of infuriating and ludicrous," Dawson said, pulling his history book out of his locker.

Pacey nodded. "Infuriating and ludicrous is my middle name. Pacey Infuriating-Ludicrous Witter. And might I add, you didn't answer the question."

Dawson slammed his locker shut. He wasn't in the best of moods. Last night, he'd rented *The English Patient*. It had been a depressing experience. For one thing, it was movie night, and it was never the same without Joey there. And for another thing, the doomed lovers in the film reminded him way too much of himself and Joey.

But at least they had some great reasons for not being together, Dawson thought. *Like that she was married to someone else. Joey and I aren't together because . . . Well, it's a very complicated because.*

And it was the worst kind of not-together. Although Joey had forgiven him, his summer in Philadelphia had changed things. He loved Joey, but he didn't want to be with her right now. Their relationship was strained, to say the least.

"This is a ridiculous conversation, Pacey," Dawson finally said. "How would you like it if I asked you to compare your love of Andie to your love of . . . of . . ." he thought a moment. "What exactly is it that you do love, Pacey? Other than Andie, I mean."

"And therein lies my problem, bro," Pacey sighed. "Minus McPhee, my life seems to lack a certain focus. Whereas yours—"

"Whereas mine lacks a certain Joey," Dawson pointed out. "What's the difference? We both acknowledge loving women we're not with. It's *Il Postino* at the beginning, classic foreign-film material—"

"Whereas you and Joey are stuck in some cliché-ridden, teen angst, on again/off again third-rate film that doesn't stand the test of time," Pacey realized.

"Actually Dawson, you're pathetic. Thanks. I feel much better."

"Great," Dawson said wryly.

They headed down the hall to their first-period class, dodging around the teeming masses of Capeside High School.

"Hey Dawson, it's so cool, huh?" Patrice Reagen called from across the hall, waving a bright red flyer in the air.

"I have absolutely no idea what she's talking about," Dawson told Pacey as they rounded the corner.

"I do," Pacey replied. "Actually, it was the stimuli for my provocative and intriguing query at your locker."

They stopped in front of Mr. Bauer's history classroom.

"It's much too early in the morning for this, Pacey. What are you talking about?"

"Hey guys," Jen Lindley called as she sidled up to them. "So, you psyched, Dawson?"

"About *what?*" Dawson asked. "What is everyone talking about?"

Pacey shook his head and sighed. "You really should consider reading the morning newspaper, Dawson. It told all."

"It's also on bright red flyers posted everywhere," Jen added, cocking her head toward the bulletin board on the opposite wall. "I have a feeling that's where Pacey got his info."

"True," Pacey admitted. "Though I *heard* it was in the morning newspaper."

3

They walked over to the bulletin board, and Dawson read the flyer posted there.

Bick Productions will be shooting the new teen horror movie *Dripping Red* in Capeside beginning next week. Seeking gofers, extras, assistants of various types. Interviews on Tuesday at the Capeside Inn 3 P.M. to 8 P.M. Bring resume, photo, all pertinent information.

"What is it, a student film?" Dawson asked. "I mean, what's the big deal about some college thing that—"

"I hate to burst your self-involved artistic bubble, Dawson," Jen said, "but it's a feature film. As in major motion picture. As in coming soon to your neighborhood cineplex."

"Really." Dawson scratched his chin. "So . . . this could be something of an opportunity."

"More than something," Pacey insisted. "Your big break. The first chapter of the tawdry tell-all novel of your life. Just remember, when you look back on these days, and you will, be kind." Pacey fluttered his eyelashes at Dawson.

Jen laughed. "How very older woman–younger man *Tea and Sympathy* of you, Pacey. But then, you'd know."

"We'll be saving that little episode of my life for *my* memoirs, thank you very much." Pacey clapped Dawson on the back. "This could be just the thing to take your mind off your appalling lack of love life."

"Gentlemen? Were you planning to join us?" Mr.

Bauer asked, sticking his head out of the classroom door.

"Absolutely," Pacey assured him.

"Sometime in this millennium would be nice," the teacher added, before disappearing back into the classroom.

"That's my cue to exit," Jen said, backing away from them. "So, we're all going for interviews tomorrow, right?"

"You're absolutely certain this isn't a student film," Dawson called to her.

"Get over it, Dawson," Jen yelled back. "The big time—meaning Bick Productions—is coming to Capeside. And the little time—meaning you—is going to beg for a job." She grinned at him. "And that about says it all."

"You want the last slice of pizza?" Dawson asked Jen, wiping some tomato sauce off his fingers.

"Three's my limit," Jen muttered, not looking up from the box of articles and papers she was sifting through on Dawson's front porch.

It was an unusually warm autumn evening. Dawson's mom, who was a television anchor woman for the local news, was working in Philadelphia. His father had moved back home, although they weren't back together.

Dawson preferred not to think about the state of his parents' marriage.

So for the time being, all he wanted in his head was preparation for an interview to work on his first professional film.

5

Dawson, Pacey, and Jen had ordered in pizza so that they could plan for their interviews for *Dripping Red*.

Jen reached in the box for another paper and peered at it by the overhead porch lights. "What did you do, Dawson? Save every single scrap of paper that was ever written about you anywhere?"

"Not every one," Dawson said. Pacey grabbed the last slice of pizza, and Dawson moved the empty box aside.

"No? Here's a note from your second-grade teacher telling your parents that after the film she showed on street safety, *Stop, Look, and Listen*, you criticized the film for being poorly directed."

"Well, it was," Dawson said defensively.

"Somehow I don't think Bick Productions will be interested in the brilliant filmic insights of eight-year-old you," Jen said dryly.

Pacey reached for an article that had been cut out of a newspaper. "But stuff like this is good. About how great your travel film selling the romance of Capeside was, *Don and Dulcie.*"

"And as producer of that film, I happen to agree," Jen said. "Look, why don't we each just write our credits up on a resume." She gestured to the box of papers. "Save this stuff for family reunions with relatives you'd like to encourage to leave quickly."

Pacey popped the last bite of pizza into his mouth. "I'll be sure to list all those starring roles I had in your early, seminal work, Dawson. What was that one called with the creature in it? The one where I was so brilliant?"

"The one where I was so desperate for an actor, but none were available, so I was forced to call for your services?" Dawson asked.

"Yeah," Pacey said. "That one."

"*Creature from the Creek,*" a familiar voice called from the darkness.

The voice came closer. Looking a lot like Joey.

"And what brings you out this fine evening?" Pacey asked. He glanced over at Dawson, then back at Joey. They were studiously avoiding each other's gaze.

"Let me amend that," Pacey said. "What brings you out this fine and extremely awkward evening?"

Joey looped some long brown hair behind one ear. "I came to talk to Jen, actually."

Jen lived with her grandmother right next door to Dawson. Which had been extremely convenient when she had first moved to Capeside from New York City, and the two of them had quickly become an item.

At least after Jen and I broke up, we stayed friends, Dawson thought. *I hope Joey and I can say that about each other someday.*

"What's up?" Jen asked Joey.

"I was hoping we could talk in private."

Jen stood up. "Ah, teen intrigue. My favorite kind." She turned to Dawson and Pacey. "I think you guys have this under control for the interview tomorrow. So I'm outta here."

The two girls headed next door to Jen's house. Dawson couldn't help but notice that neither of them gave him a backward glance.

"Frankly," Dawson began, "teen intrigue is highly overrated. I ask you, Pacey, can the people survive being best friends for years and years, then being a couple, then not a couple, then friends, then a couple, then not a couple?"

Pacey reached for the empty pizza box. "In my experience with women, anything is possible." He flung the pizza box across the lawn like a Frisbee. It smacked into a tree. "And he scores! Speaking of scoring—"

"Try to remember, Pacey, that the new and improved Witter does not mention women and scoring in the same thought pattern, and kindly unlitter my front lawn."

Pacey went after the pizza box. "You know, you've quite a talent for giving orders to lackeys, Dawson. I'd say success in the film industry is your destiny."

Jen and Joey came in through the kitchen door of Jen's house. "Want anything to drink?" Jen asked.

Joey shook her head and sat at a chair at the kitchen table. "Jack home?"

Jen shrugged. She poured herself a glass of water and sat at the table with Joey. "So?"

"Okay, I'll cut right to the chase," Joey said. "I came over because I know that while at various times our relationship has bordered on the friendly, we've never really been friends."

"And is that supposed to make sense?"

"What I'm trying to say," Joey went on, "is I know you won't lie to me under some misguided notion of friendship. And I wanted to ask you a question."

Jen drank down the last of her water. "Question away," she said.

"All right, it's like this." Joey bit her lower lip nervously. "I'm assuming you and Pacey and Dawson are all planning to interview for jobs with Bick Productions tomorrow, right?"

"Right."

"Well, I've been thinking about interviewing, too. Which leads to two more questions I wanted to ask you. Obviously Dawson will be hired in some reasonably high level to do some reasonably high level something on this film. Do you think it would be monumentally awkward if I worked on it too?"

"I think life is monumentally awkward," Jen said. "And Capeside is not exactly New York City—it's not like you and Dawson can exactly avoid each other."

"So your answer is—?"

"My answer is, Joey, that obviously that is a decision you're going to have to make for yourself. But if it's any consolation to you, he's my ex too, and I don't have any problem being around him."

Joey shot her a look. "The situations are not exactly parallel."

"True," Jen allowed. "So now that I was absolutely no help with that question, what's the other one?"

Joey hesitated. "It has to do with talent. I heard that in addition to casting extras, they're going to cast some of the smaller speaking parts locally . . ."

"And you want to know if I'm auditioning?" Jen guessed.

"No. I wanted to know if you thought I should audition."

"Meaning, do I think you have any talent? This is an interesting little guessing game, Joey," Jen added blithely. "This one I can actually answer. Yes. In my opinion, you really do have talent."

"Really?"

"No, I just said that because I was hoping that we would become bestest friends for ever and ever if I'm nice to you," Jen said.

Joey laughed. "Of all the things I've ever disliked about you, Jen, your sense of humor has never been one of them."

"Then I'll have to work harder at it," Jen cracked.

Joey got up. "So, tell Jack I said hi."

"Will do."

Jen walked Joey to the door. Joey turned back to her.

"Thanks," Joey said. "Believe it or not, that really was helpful."

Jen smiled. "Hey, what are not-friends for?"

Chapter 2

As soon as the bell rang after their last class the next day, Pacey and Dawson headed for the high school auditorium, where the interviews were being held for *Dripping Red*. Scores of kids rushed past them, toward the same destination, as if the school principal had just announced that he was giving away free beepers.

"Hey you guys," Jen said, catching up with them. "Someone just told me that the line for interviews goes out through the cafeteria already."

"But the final bell only just rang!" Dawson said.

"Some kids cut their last class to get in line early," Jen told him. "And also, every adult in town has been there for hours."

"I'm already picturing Deputy Doug, also known as older brother dearest, as Red's first victim,"

Pacey said. "Let's hope he got in line really, really early."

They rounded the corner and were greeted by the sight of an endless sea of bodies. People were everywhere—standing, sitting, kneeling, even lying down.

"It looks as if everyone in Capeside who still has a functional pulse is here," Jen remarked.

"And a few who don't," Pacey added, as he stepped over a guy who was either asleep or dead.

"But how can they possibly get through all of these people?" Dawson asked. "Doesn't it strike you as decidedly unfair to set up and conduct interviews this way?"

Jen patted his arm. "I just love it that you still expect the world to be fair, Dawson. It's really such an endearing quality."

The three of them ran smack into the end of the line.

"Excuse me," Pacey asked the girl standing in front of them. "Do you know if there's a sign-up sheet or something?"

"Some guy comes around every ten minutes and adds names to a list," the girl said. "I'm number seven thousand and two."

"Which would make me seven thousand and three," Pacey said. "And who said I couldn't do higher math?"

"What do we do now?" Dawson asked.

"Wait," Jen said. "And wait. And wait. Welcome to the big time."

*　　*　　*

"Number seven thousand and two?" a tired-sounding guy called out with a bullhorn four hours later.

"Highly amusing," Pacey said wearily as they edged forward in line.

"It is not my idea of high humor to have started the list with number six thousand seven hundred," Dawson said. "It's the type of person who enjoys making fun of peons."

"See, the difference between you and me, Dawson," Pacey began, "is that my father has been telling me that I'm a peon since the day I was born. Therefore, being treated like a peon bothers me not in the least."

"Ego strength is something Dawson can work hard to overcome," Jen joked. "Besides, you're the next warm body in there, Pacey."

"Next!" the guy called.

"That would be me," Pacey said, turning to Dawson and Jen. "Wish me luck."

"I believe the proper saying is 'break a leg,' " Jen corrected him. "And feel free not to take me literally."

Pacey was in and out of the interview in five minutes.

Jen's took ten.

Finally, it was Dawson's turn. Dawson had no idea of what had happened during his friends' interviews, because the people from the movie were sending interviewees out through a different entrance from the one they came in.

This could be it, Dawson thought as he walked

across the auditorium stage. *The defining moment when I get the major break that changes everything. I can't blow it.*

Dawson walked over to the chair up on stage. Across a small desk from him sat a short, slender guy with an alarming protruding Adam's apple, who didn't look significantly older than Dawson. The guy didn't bother to glance up when Dawson took a seat.

A flunky came over to Dawson and held out her hand. Dawson shook it. "Hello, I'm—"

"My outstretched hand meant for you to give me your resume," the girl flunky said, frostily.

"Oh, sorry," Dawson said, flustered. "I have a resume, but actually I'd like to be able to show—" he realized he had absolutely no idea of the name of the guy on the other side of the desk, who had still not looked up at him—"him, some of my clips, reviews of some of the films I've done . . ."

"And I'm sure I'd weep to see them," the young guy behind the desk said sarcastically. "Now would you please give my assistant your resume so we can get on with this?"

"Yes, sure, of course." Dawson handed her his resume.

She gave a long-suffering sigh. "This is Dawson Leery." She handed the skinny guy the resume.

"Timothy's son?" the skinny guy asked, smirking.

"Mitch's, actually," Dawson replied.

The skinny guy rolled his eyes. "I see you get no extra points for a sense of humor. So . . ." He glanced at Dawson's resume. "You've made some little filmie things?"

"Well, I like to think that they were somewhat more than little filmie things," Dawson said. "I won the junior division of the Boston Film Festival, and I—"

"I'm sure it's all right here on your most-professional professional resume," the skinny guy said. "And what is your availability for work?" His tone of voice conveyed that he couldn't care less what Dawson's availability was, but that he had to ask the question anyway.

"I'm sorry," Dawson began. "I didn't catch your name."

"I didn't throw it," the skinny guy sighed. "I would have said my name thousands of times today if I had to tell my name to every little wannabe who sat in that chair before you did, number seven thousand and five."

"With all due respect, every great film auteur started out as a wannabe at some point, didn't they?" Dawson asked.

"Oh, and did you plan to become one of them?"

"As a matter of fact," Dawson said, "yes. I've been studying film for years. My interest really began with the movie *E.T.* Since then, I've studied the greats—Orson Wells, Kurosawa, Truffaut—"

"And I would care because—?"

"Because I assumed we share a passion for film. So what's your favorite movie?"

"*A Midnight Clear,*" the skinny guy said superciliously. "Directed by Roger Gordon. But then it's not exactly Spielberg, so I'm sure you've never heard of it."

"It's a wonderful movie," Dawson said.

Don't say it, he told himself. *You know you shouldn't—*

He just couldn't help himself.

"And the director's name is *Keith* Gordon, actually," Dawson blurted out. "He directed *The Chocolate War,* too. One of my least favorite movies of all time."

Dawson added a smile as a chaser. "Sorry. I'm sure you don't like to be corrected. I mean, no one likes to be corrected."

Dawson waited for a reaction. The guy stared at him frostily, which made Dawson increasingly nervous.

"I love *The Chocolate War,*" the skinny guy finally said.

"Oh." Dawson searched his mind frantically for the right thing to say. "Well, I guess that's why they call it art."

"You're a veritable font of film knowledge, aren't you? Should I be taking notes?"

Dawson chuckled self-consciously. "I'm sorry, I know I get carried away when I talk about movies. How did you get started in the business, if you don't mind my asking?"

The skinny guy bounced the eraser end of his pencil irritably against the desk. "I could flatter you and tell you that much as I'd like to relate the story of my rise to greatness, I simply don't have time at this moment. But frankly, I have absolutely no interest in sharing it with some high school kid with delusions of film grandeur. Especially one who pontificates. Thank you so much for coming in."

Dawson rose, hesitating. "You mean, that's it?"

"That's exactly what I mean. Have a swell day. Kristin, can you call in number seven thousand and six?"

"Don't tell me, they fired the director and hired you," Patrice Reagen told Dawson. She plopped down next to him on the steps in front of the school.

"I don't know. I didn't see the list yet," Dawson replied.

It was early the next morning. They'd been told that the list of people hired to work on the film would be posted by 7:30 A.M. on the bulletin board outside the auditorium. There was a huge crowd of people outside the high school doors, because the custodians hadn't yet unlocked the building.

The list would be posted in ten minutes.

After his abysmal interview, Dawson did not have a good feeling about it.

I should have kept my mouth shut, Dawson told himself for perhaps the hundredth time. *I shouldn't have corrected that insecure, nasty little guy who interviewed me. I shouldn't have—*

"Well, everyone knows that you know more about film than anyone in Capeside," Patrice pointed out, interrupting Dawson's silent regrets.

"You probably know more about film than anyone in the state of Massachusetts."

Flattered, he temporarily put his thoughts about his terrible interview aside and smiled at her. She smiled back.

Funny how he'd never noticed before how pretty she was. The early morning sun glinted off her glossy auburn hair and lightly freckled nose.

Of course, she's no Joey, Dawson thought. But I have to stop comparing every single girl I meet to Joey. That's like asking for a lifetime of pain.

And celibacy.

"I didn't know that you were interested in movies," Dawson said.

She shrugged. "I'm a teenager. I heard it's illegal not to be interested."

"I meant you haven't taken any film classes here, have you?"

Patrice shook her head. "I've been kind of too busy with other stuff."

"Like what?"

She looked kind of sheepish. "Well, I'm kind of into . . . comic strips."

"What, you mean like *Doonesbury*? *Peanuts*?"

"Not exactly. I design my own strip, actually. It's called GLIB, which stands for Girl's Life Isn't Bliss. Sort of teen girl angst meets *Xena*."

Dawson laughed. "That sounds fantastic. Sort of *Daria* with a sword?"

It was her turn to laugh. "Something like that." She cocked her head at him. "I have to admit, Dawson, I never knew you had an actual sense of humor."

And I never knew you at all, Dawson thought. *It's so amazing how you can see someone day after day and not really see them at all.*

"So, is your strip for public consumption?" Dawson asked her.

"Oh, sure," she said breezily. "I figure my real insanity shines through in every panel, so people who hate my strip are gonna hate me, too. It saves a lot of time."

As she reached into her backpack for her sketch pad, Dawson couldn't help compare her open attitude about showing him her art to Joey's attitude about showing hers.

Patrice seemed like a breath of fresh air.

She handed her art pad to Dawson.

He flipped it open. There were pages and pages of cartoons starring a girl with wild auburn curls and freckles on her nose, who looked a lot like Patrice. But instead of wielding a sword as a weapon, she would zap people into silence with the magic rays from the bottom of her platform sandals.

"These are fantastic!" Dawson told her.

"You think?" she asked, looking pleased by his reaction.

"Absolutely. Have you tried to get them published?"

"Only in the school paper," Patrice replied. "But I used to go out with the editor in chief, and he's a complete butthole who never got over me dropping him, so he refuses to run the strip."

Dawson handed the sketch pad back to her. "You

should just post them on the Internet," he suggested. "I bet you'll get a million hits."

She beamed at him. "You know, that's actually a fantastic idea."

Dawson saw her eyes slide to a group of people standing near the flagpole, one of whom was Joey.

"You and Joey Potter are a thing, aren't you?" she asked him.

"We're . . . it's hard to say exactly what we are."

"In like? In love? In lust? All of the above?" Patrice asked.

Dawson looked uncomfortable. He had absolutely no idea how to answer her question.

"Or, I could zap you with the bottoms of my platform sandals so you don't have to answer the question," she offered.

"It's complicated—" Dawson began.

The people standing outside the doors surged inside, and the other kids down by the flagpole suddenly headed for the building.

"Hey, they just unlocked the doors!" someone yelled.

"Well, I guess that's our cue," Patrice said, as she rose to her feet.

Dawson got up, too. "I really enjoyed talking with you."

"Me too." Patrice dropped her sketch pad into her backpack. "And who knows? Maybe we can do more than talk sometime."

Before Dawson could formulate a response to that, Patrice had rushed inside the school.

*   *   *

The crowd around the bulletin board outside the auditorium was so huge that it was impossible for Dawson to see the list.

"Psyche! I'm a movie star!" someone yelled.

"Get a grip, you're an extra," someone else yelled.

Dawson spotted Pacey further up in the crowd and worked his way over to him. "Did you see the list yet?"

"No, but I'm just preparing to mow down these lowly freshmen so I can see what's up there," Pacey replied. "Shall we mow?"

"We shall," Dawson replied with false bravado, and they worked their bodies up toward the list.

So maybe I won't get a great job, Dawson thought. *But they can't give me no job at all.*

They ran into Jen and Joey.

"Greetings from the new assistant to the assistant producer," Jen told them happily.

Dawson gave her a quick hug. "I'm so happy for you, Jen, that's great, really."

"So, Joey, are you on the list?" Dawson asked her.

She nodded. "I'm an extra. So are you, Pacey. Catch you later," she added and hurried off.

Like I have a communicable disease, Dawson thought sadly. Sometimes he wondered if Joey knew how much it hurt to know she was hurting.

"Don't look so pained, Dawson," Jen said. "Wearing your heart on your sleeve is distinctly out of style."

"Frankly, the only thing on my mind is what position I got on the picture," Dawson lied. He pushed forward close enough so that he could see the list. His eyes scanned it with a combination of anticipation and dread.

There was an endless list of names. Extras. Gofers. Assistants of every type he had ever imagined, and many types he had never imagined.

He found the names of just about everyone he knew.

What he couldn't find was his own name.

Anywhere.

He felt Jen's arms snake around his waist from behind. "So, Dawson, what did Arnie Bick give you?"

His eyes went to the top of the list again. It just couldn't be true.

"Who's Arnie Bick?" Dawson asked distractedly.

"The associate producer, the guy who interviewed you."

Dawson turned to her. "Arnie Bick? As in Bick Productions?"

"Come on, Dawson," Jen said, as they worked their way out of the crowd. "You knew who he was."

"No, actually, I had no idea who he was. He refused to tell me his name."

Pacey followed them out of the crowd. "Who, the little weenie with an Adam's apple the size of the Indianapolis Motor Speedway, who interviewed us? He wouldn't tell me his name, either."

Jen grinned. "Clearly, I made a massive impression on him, then. So really, Dawson, what did you get?"

The word "nothing" came to his lips, but it was just so horrible he couldn't push it out of his mouth.

"You know, I actually think I need to check the list again," was what came out, instead.

But he knew he could check the list every hour on the hour for the rest of his life, and his name still was not going to be there.

Chapter 3

Jack McPhee sat on Jen's bed and watched her as
she combed her hair, her eyes fixed on her own re-
flection in the mirror above her dresser.

"Interesting outfit for your first day working on a
movie titled *Dripping Red*," he noted, taking in
Jen's bright red T-shirt and black jeans. "Planning to
continue the red motif in your lipstick, earrings,
tasteful baby barettes?"

"Consider the color of my T-shirt a coincidence."
Jen turned around and leaned against her dresser. "I
still don't see why you didn't want to try to work on
the movie."

"It's a little thing called school, Jen. And another
little thing called football practice. And football
games. Last time I looked, Coach Mitch wasn't giving excused absences to work in movies."

Jack had moved in with Jen and her grandmother after his sister Andie had gone to the Mayfield Care Center. And though Andie had returned to Capeside, to live with her father, Jack decided to stay with Jen and her Grams. Jen really liked having Jack living at her house, so she was thrilled when he decided to stay.

She walked toward the bed and sat down next to him.

"You know my grandmother and I love having you live here," Jen began.

"Almost like a girlfriend, huh?" Jack asked, a half-smile on his face.

"Not quite. And please do not make jokes at my friend Jack's expense."

Jack stretched his arms and rested them behind his head. "I can appreciate a good homo joke, even if it is at my expense. For example, yesterday, Pacey asked me when I was going to ask his brother Doug out. I told him I was holding out for senior prom."

Jen laughed. "I knew there was a reason I liked having you around. You're funny."

"Well, it's a good thing I'm amusing," Jack mused aloud, "because I'm also broke. But Jack-the-charity-case gets a little old."

"Butt is what you're a pain in, you know that?" Jen gave him a quick hug, then stood up. "Well, I'm off for day one of my first job on a professional film. Wish me luck."

Jack got up, too. "Good luck, but you won't need it. You'll be great. Maybe I'll stop over at Dawson's and see if he's still licking his wounds."

Jen slung her backpack over one shoulder. "I still can't believe they didn't give him any kind of gig on this movie. I mean, I feel like a fraud. He's the one who introduced me to film, he's the one who taught me everything I know. Yet he's out, and I'm in."

Jack smiled. "Well, if you had planned it, I'd say how very *All About Eve* of you."

"But that's just it," Jen said. "I didn't plan it. I didn't even wish it. In fact, I wish there was somebody I could tell about the mammoth mistake they've made by not giving him a job on their movie."

"So, just out of curiosity, would those feelings stem from friendship, or something more than friendship?" Jack asked.

"Why Jack, what a girlfriend-ish question for you to pose," Jen teased. She thought a moment. "You know, the truth is, I have absolutely no idea what the truth is. I sometimes wonder if Dawson and I might be a story to be continued. But truthfully, I believe he and Joey are soulmates."

"Funny how Dawson seems to get all the women I love," Jack noted wryly.

"Cheer up, Jack, look at it this way: my Grams would never let Dawson Leery live here!"

"Jen! Jen Lindley, isn't it?"

Arnold Bick rushed toward Jen, his arms open wide, as if she were a long-lost relative. He enveloped her in a bearhug, then held her at arm's length by the shoulders. "Just because I'm your boss and you're my assistant, I want you to know I don't stand on ceremony, Jen. Please, call me Arnie."

Jen smoothly stepped away so that Arnie's hands dropped to his sides. "Great, I appreciate a relaxed work environment."

They were in the trailer that served as one of the production offices. It was set up near the docks. Two others just like it had been placed nearby.

Arnie draped an arm around one of Jen's shoulders. "Right over here is your desk. See all the little pencils in the cup? I had them sharpened for you."

"How thoughtful." Jen slipped out from under his arm.

He frowned at her. "Jen, may I ask you a personal question?"

She folded her arms. "You may ask, but that doesn't mean I have to answer."

Arnie laughed, as if she had just told the world's greatest joke. "Okay, here's my question. Are you one of those uptight people who don't like to be touched? I'm only asking because I'm a very loving, demonstrative, physical-type guy. I've been in show business all of my life. And we're all very loving, demonstrative, physical-type people."

"Well, my loving, demonstrative, physical-type response to that is . . . wait a minute. Before I answer that, how old are you, anyway? If you don't mind my asking."

"My life is an open book, Jen," Arnie said, throwing his arms open wide. "I'm twenty-one. But I've always been wise beyond my years. Therapy, you know."

"Right." Jen was beginning to get a headache directly between her eyes.

She had already nicknamed the headache "Arnie."

"Well, as you know from my interview, I'm sixteen. You know, as in a *minor*."

He threw his arms open again. "That's only a *minor* problem, then!" He laughed, and it was a cross between a bray and a cackle. He amused himself so much that it took him a moment to catch his breath. "Sorry, sorry." He wiped tears of mirth from his eyes. "So, where were we? You didn't answer my question before."

"Let's just say that I'm perfectly capable of being loving, demonstrative, and exhibiting a physical-type response . . . with the proper person, at the proper time. And since you've been a professional for twenty-one years now, I'm sure you realize that this is neither the time nor the place."

He wagged a finger at her, a twinkle in his eye. "You're good, you're very, very good."

"And you're very, very quoting *Analyze This*," Jen noted.

He nodded. "Ya got me. But that's just how I am. I love the cinema. Almost as much as I love women. Sue me."

I won't be suing you anytime soon, Arnie, because if I sued you I won't be getting the measly paycheck I've been promised, Jen thought.

She walked over and sat behind the desk, thinking that putting the maximum amount of distance between her and Arnie Bick was a good idea. "So, Arnie, where would you like me to begin?"

He thought a moment. "Go make me some coffee. Half-regular, half-decaf, two Equals, and a tablespoon of Kreamarino powder—love the stuff, so don't skimp. Tastes like milk, made from soy byproducts. Amazing. No milk under any circumstances for me. I'm lactose intolerant. Thanks, Jen, babe. You're a doll."

Two hours later, Joey checked her watch for maybe the tenth time in the past hour. She was standing on the beach with a few dozen other extras, all of them clad in beach wear. They were all waiting for someone or other to tell them to do something or other.

So far, all that had happened was that an assistant named Serena had bitched at them to please stand there, shut up, and wait.

Meanwhile, thirty yards away, a crew had been working at erecting a camera tower on the beach. They were having a lot of trouble anchoring it in the sand.

It had fallen over twice, and they were now on their third effort.

"Joey, Joey, Joey," Pacey crooned, ambling over to her. "You're looking delightful in your swimwear."

"And I'm feeling mighty delightful, too."

Joey looked Pacey over from head to toe, squinting in the bright sunshine. "Just out of curiosity, Pacey, when you bought those neon surfer jams, did those sunglasses come with them? To protect the eyes of your friends who have to look at you?"

"It's a little mix-and-match ensemble I kind of put

together," Pacey replied easily. "The sunglasses are so my fans don't mob me."

"And so far, you've been a complete success. Where have you been for the past two hours?"

"Discussing life, love, and the pursuit of happiness, with Emily LaPaz. Down by the waterline."

Joey nodded with feigned seriousness. "And here I assumed you were discussing how magnanimous it was for someone as studly as you to have accepted the role of 'beach scene extra.' "

"As you travel down the thespian highway, Joey, let these words be your guide: there are no small parts, there are only small—"

"Parts that fit into neon yellow surfer jams," Joey said sweetly. "Not to demean your manhood, Pacey, but those are the baggiest jams I've ever seen. Where are you hiding your . . . shins?"

He put his hands to his heart. "You wound me. Don't you know a hip happening *Boyz 'N the Hood* gangsta rap artiste look when you see one?"

"Right. Pacey Witter *is* Ice Pee."

Pacey did a couple of quick moves in the sand he had seen Snoop Doggy Dog do in a video.

"Pacey, as a long-time friend—at least a long time acquaintance—I have to tell you that, on you, those moves are frightening."

"Excellent. As we are appearing in a horror movie."

Joey looked at her watch again. "At this rate, we aren't appearing in anything. This is the very first day of shooting, and there has been a decided lack of shooting. So far, all we've done is—"

"People! May I have your attention?"

A voice boomed out so loudly it sounded as if it was coming from the heavens.

Joey and Pacey turned toward the source of the voice: a sound truck that was now parked further up the beach. A person they recognized stood in front of the sound truck, holding a microphone.

"For those of you who don't know me," the figure said, his voice heavily amplified, "I'm the associate producer of this picture, Mr. Arnold Bick."

"How could we not know him?" Joey hissed at Pacey. "He's the one who interviewed all of us. In fact, he asked me if I was a loving, demonstrative, physical-type person. Did he ask you that?"

"Why do I think that how you fill out that bathing suit and how I fill out these jams have something to do with the fact that no, he did not ask me that," Pacey replied dryly.

"For those of you who are new to the magic of moviemaking," Arnie went on, "let me just say that time is money and art is everything."

"Profound," Pacey said.

"And now, with no further ado, it is my great pleasure and distinct honor to introduce you to the auteur of this film, Mr.—the legendary—Reginald London the Third."

Pacey took off his sunglasses. "Let's give it up for Reggie!" he whooped, swinging his arm in a circle. "Reg-gie, Reg-gie, Reg-gie!"

No one joined in. Pacey hastily put his sunglasses back on.

A man sitting in a tall canvas director's chair, atop

the sound truck, waved one hand in the air like Saddam Hussein. He wore an impeccable white suit and a white Panama hat pulled down low. Wraparound Ray-Bans shielded his eyes. Arnie tossed the microphone to a flunky, who, in turn, tossed it up to the director.

Reginald caught it neatly.

"The first day of a film is always the most exciting for me," Reginald's voice boomed out, deeper than Arnie's. "It's a spiritual thing, which is why I always like to start out with a moment of meditation to bring us all together. Please, join hands with those nearest you."

"*Creek Daze* is starting to look really good to me," Joey muttered, but she dutifully held her hand out to Pacey.

"You're beautiful," Pacey said, grabbing her hand and pretending to sniff back copious tears.

"Now, everyone, close your eyes," Reginald instructed. "I want you to think about this day. This moment. Let all the muses of the heavens shine upon us, and upon our film."

He closed his eyes and bowed his head.

"This is like, a joke, right?" a fat kid on the other side of Joey wondered aloud, hiking his gym shorts up with the hand that wasn't holding Joey's.

Joey snuck one eye open. All the way down the beach, people of all sizes and shapes, in bathing suits, had their eyes closed and their heads bowed. It was as if Hands Across America had come back again for *Hands Across America II: On the Beach.*

Reginald lifted his head, and his eyes popped open. "All right! I feel cleansed! I'm sure you do, too. Films are not shot in order. So today, we'll be doing some happy-happy-happy beach scenes that occur about ten minutes into my movie. The stars won't be arriving until tomorrow."

He tossed the microphone back to the flunky below, who handed it to a cute young guy in jeans and a Hawaiian shirt, who wore a lightweight wireless headset with earphone and mike.

"My name is Ken Latham," the guy said. "I'm the first assistant director. I'll be the one giving you your cues. First, I'll tell you what the attitude should be in the scene we're about to shoot, and then, just like in the movies, when I call 'action,' you act."

A hand attached to a tall girl in a thong bikini waved wildly in the crowd.

"This isn't school, you don't have to raise your hand," Ken said easily. "What's up?"

"Well, what I would like to know," thong bikini began, "is, are we supposed to like make up our own character and then talk to people in that character, or what?"

"Yeah, that's exactly what you do," Ken replied. "And actually, we dub the sound in later. But you never know. Maybe we'll use what you say."

A thrilled titter went through the crowd on the beach.

Joey looked at Pacey. "This town is hard up for excitement."

Ken looked up at Reginald. "We about ready for

the first shot? The guys on the tower gave me the okay over my headset."

"Fantastic! I love the light, right now. Very evocative," Reginald said, eyes narrowed.

Ken spoke into the mike again, addressing the extras.

"Okay, you're happy, you're having fun, it's a typical summer day at the beach in Capeside," he instructed. "You don't know anything about any psycho named Red, who drips a trail of blood behind him after each killing. When Serena calls for action, do what you'll do in the scene, so Reggie can get a sense of how things are going to go."

A blood-curdling scream was emitted from tall, thin, thong bikini. She looked at Ken, her eyes hopeful.

"Just in case you need another victim," she offered.

"Happy People on the Beach Scene, Rehearsal for Take One," Serena called out in her permanently grumpy voice. "Action!"

All up and down the beach, the extras went into action. Some unfolded blankets and plopped down on them, some started tossing Frisbees, others ran down the beach toward the pounding surf.

By the sound truck, Arnie looked around for Jen. "Jen!" he called. "Jen Lindley!"

Jen, who was standing on the shady side of the truck, heard him calling her.

"Yes?" she said, coming around the truck toward the sound of his voice.

"Iced coffee!" Arnie commanded. "More Kreamarino this time."

"I should have asked for a job description," Jen muttered under her breath.

"Okay, be right back!" she called to Arnie, and turned to head off to the catering area.

She practically smacked into Ken Latham, the assistant director.

"Hi," Ken said with a laugh. "Be careful. We've got enough dead bodies coming up in this movie."

"Sorry," Jen explained, "but Arnie—"

"I know all about it. Lots of Kreamarino," Ken broke in. "Don't skimp."

Jen smiled, and Ken put out his hand. "I'm Ken Latham, the assistant director."

Jen shook it. "Jen Lindley, assistant to—"

"Arnie," Ken filled in. "Which makes you a saint if you've already lasted this long. Welcome aboard the movie."

Ken flashed a smile so warm and friendly that, at least for the moment, made Jen forget all about Arnie Bick and his penchant for Kreamarino.

Chapter 4

Dawson paced the sidewalk at the edge of the beach directly across the street from the ice cream parlor. Which is exactly what he had been doing for the past three hours. Every fifteen minutes or so he'd get as close as he could to the movie set and watch what was happening. Then, when he couldn't stand it any longer, he went back to his sidewalk.

He just couldn't believe what had happened. This was the second day of shooting, all of his friends were involved in it, the whole stupid town of Capeside was involved in it, but Dawson Leery was not.

In one way, I know it's my fault. I knew I should have kept my mouth shut in that interview. I could tell that his ego was roughly ten times the size of his Adam's apple. Which is roughly ten times the size of his knowledge of film, Dawson thought. *But I just couldn't help myself.*

He swung around, ready to head back to get close to the set again—it was like some kind of masochistic exercise that he kept repeating—when someone called to him from the doorway of the ice cream parlor.

"Hey Dawson! I hope you're clocking your mileage, because I have a feeling you've roughly walked the Boston Marathon in the past few hours."

Dawson turned around. Patrice Reagen was grinning at him, her sketch pad tucked under one arm.

It surprised him how glad he was to see her. He crossed the street to her.

"I thought you were working on the movie," he said.

"Zero interest."

Dawson looked puzzled. "But you were at school so early that morning—"

"And you figured the only reason anyone would be at school that early would be to see if they got hired?"

"That seemed like a logical deduction," Dawson replied.

"Well, deduce this. You were wrong." She pushed some curls out of her eyes. In the bright early afternoon sunlight, Dawson could see all the various shades of red and gold in her auburn hair.

Like autumn leaves, he thought. That one week

when the colors are so perfect that you wish it could last forever.

"So, are you interested in a triple-dip chocolate chip, with sprinkles? My treat," Patrice offered.

"Thanks, but watching the movie shoot without my involvement in it has made me lose my appetite. It might be permanent."

"Well, let's at least sit down at a table. You can lick your wounds, and I can lick a cone. Be right back."

Patrice dashed inside the parlor, and Dawson sat down at one of the wrought-iron tables on the sidewalk outside. Moments later, Patrice came out holding two cones. She held one out to him. "I swear, scientific research has shown that the antidote to depression is really high-fat ice cream."

Patrice sat down across from him, and they silently munched on their cones for a while. And for the first time since Dawson had seen that his name was not on the list for the movie, he felt almost human.

"So, I'm curious, what were you doing at school that early?" Dawson asked.

She wiggled her eyebrows. "I'm a woman of mystery. Meaning I'm not telling."

Dawson laughed. "That reply is pretty much a guarantee that I'll be so curious that I'll keep on asking."

"All right, I can't take it anymore," Patrice cried dramatically. "You've forced me to tell you!"

She leaned close to him, glanced in both directions as if to make sure that no secret agent was eavesdropping, and then said, conspiratorially, "I came because I knew you'd be there."

Dawson was stunned. Beyond stunned, actually. He couldn't have been more stunned if someone had told that, say, Quentin Tarentino had showed up at his front door and told him that there was no need to finish high school; won't Dawson come to Hollywood, immediately, to be his personal protégé?

"On the list of natural bodily functions that I do well, I had in the past always thought that hearing was right up there," Dawson told her. "I could swear that you just said you were at school that early because—"

Patrice nodded, and popped the last of her ice cream cone into her mouth.

"Well . . . I'm flattered," Dawson admitted. "No, I'm . . . more than flattered. I'm . . . the truth is I'm . . . flabbergasted."

"Flabbergasted," Patrice said, rolling the word around in her mouth. "What a great word. Where do you think it comes from? Flabber-gasted. It's sort of like *Flubber* meets *Blazing Saddles.*"

"Interesting imagery," Dawson said, "but I have to admit that I'm not following you."

"You know, *Blazing Saddles.* The campfire scene. The *beans.* Flubber-gasted. My father rents these gems. I try to avoid them."

When Dawson realized what she was talking about, he laughed so hard that tears came to his eyes. This girl was *funny.* And smart. She'd made a joke about films. Old films.

And best of all, he thought, she seems to really like me. And he genuinely liked her.

"Done any more GLIB cartoons lately?" Dawson asked.

"You remember the title of my strip, Dawson. I'm touched. Yeah, I work on it every day. It's like my obsession."

"I know exactly what that feels like. That's how I am about movies."

"And it really bites the big one," Patrice noted, "that there's a movie being shot not six hundred feet from us, and they've shut you out completely. Hard to fathom, by the by."

Dawson winced, as his dreadful interview flashed through his mind again. "Let's just say it's a case of cause and effect."

Patrice glanced at her watch, frowned, and stood up. "I gotta run. Say, did you hear about the party at Chris Wolfe's tonight?"

Dawson stood, also. "No."

"Yeah, for everyone who's working on the movie. He told me that the stars who flew in are going to be there, too."

"Stars?" Dawson echoed, his voice withering. "Did Laurence Olivier come back from the great beyond to play the definitive role of a lifetime, Mr. Dripping Red?"

"You know the psycho in these movies is always someone completely unknown," Patrice chided him playfully. "And the people who get killed off early always have the fewest credits, the worst agents, and the best anatomical parts that money can buy. I'm talking about stars like Laken Whitt, Melissa Reynolds, and Burk Flint."

"Laken Whitt's last picture was a direct-to-video tenth-rate cheese-fest called *Girls' Dorm at Midnight,*" Dawson sneered. "Melissa Reynolds did have that pivotal career-making moment when she guest starred on *Saved By the Bell,* which was a step up from her film career to date—and I do use the term loosely—in *Roller Babes from Hell . . .*"

Patrice grinned. "You really do know film. Especially of the four-star cheese-fest sort," she teased. "And what pearls of dis-dom do you have for Burk Flint?"

"He was reasonably acceptable in his one and only film, *Mega Hurts,*" Dawson grudgingly admitted.

"As Mega's boyfriend, the one guy who finally got her over her fear of commitment," Patrice rhapsodized. "Because he was so sensitive, so intelligent, so perfectly cut when he ripped off his shirt."

"And that is all too often, sadly, what passes for talent in Hollywood these days."

"The truth is, Dawson, my heart pitter-patters much more for Lynda Barry comic strips and vintage R. Crumb than twenty-foot-high pecs on the silver screen. So, you wanna go?"

"Go?"

"Try to keep up, Dawson. To Chris Wolfe's party tonight," Patrice said. "With me."

"Meaning you are asking me out?"

"I like a guy who catches on so quickly," Patrice quipped. "And your answer would be?"

"My answer would be . . ." Dawson's voice trailed off.

"Ouch. I was hoping for an instantaneous positive reinforcement. Say, you jumping up and down, turning cartwheels. Or at least a resounding yes."

"The part about you asking me out, in and of itself, merits a resounding yes," Dawson assured her. "The part about going to a party involved with the film, with which I'm not involved, is what makes me hesitate."

She grabbed his hand and beamed at him. "Oh, what the hell, Dawson, let's live dangerously. Is there a better way for you to show how little you think of their pathetic excuse for a movie than to pretend you don't care?"

"No. But—"

"Then it's settled." Patrice began to back away from him. "I gotta tell you, Dawson, you are really cute when you lie so badly. Pick you up at eight."

Chapter 5

By the time Jen and Jack arrived at Chris Wolfe's house for the party that night, the place was already hopping. Conveniently, his parents were out of town, so no place in his palatial home, complete with swimming pool and hot tub, was off-limits to the partiers. And it was clear to Jen that they were already making use of each and every inch of space.

Four girls in postage stamp–size bikinis frolicked in the hot tub, with two college-aged guys Jen knew were production assistants of some sort. A bunch of couples, Chris Wolfe and his latest soon-to-be-conquest among them, were chicken-fighting in the heated swimming pool, the girls sitting on the guys' shoulders. Rap music blared out of a tasty sound system on the patio, where two dozen or so people were dancing.

"Quite the bash," Jack noted, taking in the scene.

"Why do I feel like I just walked into a scene from *Can't Hardly Wait*?" Jen asked, bemused.

"That's one of the many movies I didn't see and have no regrets about not seeing," Jack replied. "And I have a feeling, Jen, that this is one of the parties I would have been better off not attending."

Jen took his arm. "Oh, come on, Jack, try at least to pretend that you're a teenager with minor banal teenage type things on your mind. You know, sex, drugs, rock and roll, raging hormones, all that."

"The truth is, I came because you asked me to come with you," Jack reminded her.

She kissed him on the cheek. "And I appreciate it, Jack. Frankly, I'd rather be with you than with almost any guy I know."

Jen's gaze landed on Ken, who was talking to one of the more spectacular-looking extras near the sliding glass doors to the patio.

In the two days she'd spent working on the film so far, she had to admit that she already liked Ken Latham. A lot. It wasn't just that he was so cute—although he was—with his dark hair, light blue eyes, and a Freddy Prinze Jr.–type physique. He was also smart, really nice, funny, and he treated even the lowliest gofer with respect and consideration.

She had begun to envy his assistant, who, she couldn't help noticing, actually got to do things instead of spending her time shuttling Kreamerino-laden coffee to and from her boss.

She also couldn't help but notice that Ken was doing about eighty percent of the real work of directing. In fact, although her frame of reference was admittedly limited, it seemed to her that Reginald London III had not had one unique or even decent idea since the picture had started shooting.

Jack's eyes followed hers. "Is that him?" He cocked his head toward Ken.

She had told Jack all about Ken the night before, when she'd come home from the set.

Jen nodded. "What do you think?"

"I think he couldn't possibly be good enough for you, and it's time for me to be a manly man and fight him for the honor of your favors," Jack joshed.

"I'm proud of you, Jack. You're letting your playful side out. Next thing you know, you'll be hanging out at midnight showings of the *Rocky Horror Picture Show,* dressed like Magenta."

"Who's Magenta?"

Jen shook her head. "Never mind. Should we get something to drink?"

"Actually, Jen, your latest victim is heading this way," Jack noted. "Which is why I'm going off to find something to drink, and you're going to stand here and radiate femme fatale appeal."

Jack ambled off toward the house, as Ken made his way over to Jen.

"Hey. I was hoping you'd show," Ken said.

"It's a wonderful thing in life, when hope turns into reality, isn't it?" Jen regarded him coolly.

The truth was, she didn't really feel very cool at all. She had tried on half of her closet trying to decide what to wear to the party, because she knew that Ken would be there. She'd finally settled on khakis and her favorite white sheer blouse from a little SoHo boutique that she'd bought back in the days when she had known the joys of credit cards and her father's open checkbook. And, of course, over that she'd thrown on her lucky leather jacket.

Sexy, but insouciant, she hoped. Her eyes slid over to him, and she wondered how old he was. He had to be out of college. Which would make him what Grams would surely call "shockingly too old" for her.

But then, she and Grams didn't exactly see eye-to-eye on most things regarding guys.

"Oh, I don't know," Ken mused. "Sometimes hoping is the best part, and reality is a big disappointment."

Jen laughed. "Said like a man with either a deep Peter Pan complex or a deep need to get into the movie business."

"The latter. I hope. So, how's it going working for Arnie?"

"I can't say I ever in my life met anyone who actually consumed Kreamerino," Jen admitted. "He swallows so much of that stuff you'd think he owned stock in the company."

"Between me and you, his family is so rich he doesn't have to worry about owning stock in anything," Ken confided.

Jen's eyebrows shot up. "Let's see . . . Bick Productions, Arnold Bick. Coincidence?"

They said at exactly the same time, "I think not."

They both laughed.

"So, what's up with that?" Jen asked.

Ken scratched his chin. "I think it goes something like this. Arnie's father and uncle made a fortune in the shoe business. Murray and Myrtle Shoes? That's them. So when Arnie's first cousin, Mike, graduated from film school, the shoe bros basically purchased him a film production company."

"That's quite the graduation present," Jen noted.

"Well, at least Mike Bick actually has talent—he's the exec producing this project. Plus, he's a nice guy. Neither of which I can really say about the Arnster."

Jen nodded her agreement. "Two days of making his coffee and I already feel like my life is passing before my eyes on a continual basis, plus he has this touchy-feelie thing he does—"

"Believe me, you're not the first assistant to the assistant producer to voice that complaint," Ken told her. "This is the third Bick production I've worked on. And, by some strange alignment of the stars, all of Arnie's assistants are young, gorgeous, and female. Coincidence?"

Together they said, "I think not."

Jen smiled up at him flirtatiously. "So, it's fair to assume that you were just tossing me a compliment?"

"Absolutely. Although since it involves working for Arnie, I also have to add my condolences. And listen, seriously, if the guy touches you, or goes too far in any way, let me know."

"Gee, I feel all girly and breathless," Jen said sarcastically.

Ken shrugged. "Just trying to help. Hey, you're only, what, sixteen?"

"I realize you don't know anything about me," Jen said. "I'm not from Capeside. I'm a New Yorker. We have the sex harassment laws memorized by the time we hit puberty."

"Good. Because I assume that makes you extremely mature for your tender years," Ken said.

"I was born mature." Jen studied him a moment. "You're flirting with me, right?"

He smiled.

"Yeah, that's another thing about us New York girls: excellent flirting radar."

"Still," Ken began, "sixteen is only sixteen—"

"Pretend it's in dog years," Jen suggested. "Which would make me, roughly, a hundred and twenty."

"And extremely well-preserved for your age, I might add."

"Thank you. And now, you'd better dance with me," Jen said. "You never know, at my age, this might be the last dance I get."

He put out an arm. Jen took it, and he led her to the patio.

Joey ambled over to Pacey. He was leaning against a wall in the family room, watching the action swirl around him.

"Holding up the house, Pacey?" Joey asked.

"Just observing the mating rituals of the young and carefree," Pacey replied. "At the moment, I'm wallowing in adolescent angst."

"Don't tell me. Its initials are A.M."

"Precisely. Do you know that not a day goes by, Joey, that I don't say to myself, 'What would Andie have thought of that?' Or, 'Oh, Andie would think that's so funny, I have to tell Andie.' And then I realize, all over again, that I can't because it's over. We're over."

Joey patted his arm. "It doesn't have to be."

"Yes, it does," he replied firmly. "For now at least. I have to make sure that I can still be me without—"

"Pacey, I've known you my entire life. Remember?" Joey interrupted. "I know you think Andie made your life better. I think she did too. But the person you are now, the one you became, the one you will be—well, you are responsible for that."

He grabbed her arm dramatically. "You're beautiful, Joey Potter. And I mean that with all sincerity. Now, if all the beautiful girls on the beach would please jump up and down when you hear 'action!' "

Joey chuckled. It was obvious that Pacey was imitating the one-and-only Reginald London III, who had spent most of the day asking all the female extras in the beach scene to jump up and down. He had even asked that a trampoline be brought in, but Ken had pretended that they couldn't find one in all of Capeside.

"That guy has the least talent and the most sexist attitude of anyone I ever met in my entire life," Joey fumed.

"Might I point out that the only director you've ever worked for has been the illustrious D. Leery?"

"Well," Joey said, "I'm sure there are plenty of talented directors around. And who do not consider an overdeveloped girl bouncing on a trampoline the epitome of art."

"Joey, Joey, Joey," Pacey sighed. "They are, alas, few and far between. Most directors are about on the psychosocial development level of Reginald London."

"Did I just hear you talking about Reginald?" a girl passing by them stopped to ask.

Pacey had seen the girl sitting in a canvas chair near one of the production trailers. But he had no idea who she was. At the time she had been laughing at something that one of the gofers was saying, and he had noticed that she had one of the sweetest smiles he had ever seen.

She was totally opposite Andie in looks. Short, curvy, with dark hair and eyes. And great dimples.

"Ah yes," he said. "Reginald. The third. It gives one pause to think about who the first and the second might have been."

He held out a hand to her. "I'm Pacey Witter, lowly extra. And this is my friend Joey Potter, ditto."

The girl shook Pacey's hand, then Joey's. "Laken Whitt," she said. "I get killed near the end when Red drips me to death. I suffocate on his blood."

"Artistic," Joey commented. "Who wrote this screenplay again?"

"Well, on the copy of the screenplay I have," Laken said, "it says it's by someone named Lewis Montgomery. But I heard the actual last name is Bick. Which one, I don't know. But hey, it's a gig. It beats doing *Girls' Dorm at Midnight, II*."

"Sorry," Joey admitted. "I never saw *Girl's Dorm, I.*"

"Consider yourself fortunate. Hey, it's work. And I got my SAG card that way. Screen Actors Guild," Laken explained. "Great health insurance."

"So what you're telling us is that, for you, this movie represents a career move," Pacey deduced.

Laken made a face. "Gee, when you put it like that, I could get really depressed. And so could my parents, who paid for me to go to Yale."

Joey grew wide-eyed. "Really? You went to Yale?"

"No, I went to Southwestern Missouri State for a semester," Laken admitted. "Then I dropped out and went to Hollywood seeking fame and fortune. I just wanted to see if you'd buy it. And you did!"

"A brilliant performance," Pacey said earnestly. "I wept."

"To tell you the truth, the thing I really love, and the thing I'm best at, is improv," she told them.

Joey and Pacey looked at her blankly.

"Improv? You know, as in, improvisational comedy. Make it up while you're doing it, Second City, the Groundlings, *Whose Line Is It Anyway?*"

"Oh, that kind of improv," Pacey said. "Of course, we know all about that kind of improv."

Joey shot him a look. "Liar."

"True," Pacey admitted. "I just wanted to see if she'd buy it."

"I have a feeling you'd do really well in Hollywood," Laken told him, "it's the bull capital of the world. So, are there any comedy clubs in Capeside?"

"Just the usual amusement of 8 A.M. to 3 P.M. commonly known as Capeside High," Joey told her.

Laken shook her head and shuddered. "High school was the worst. So, I've been talking to some of the other people in the cast about getting together tomorrow night to do some improv. If you're up for it?"

"Where?" Joey asked.

"We're all staying at the Capeside Inn," Laken said. "So, someplace there. I'll let you know. You guys in?"

"Not me," Pacey said quickly. "I have enough trouble thinking up what to say when I give myself more time than anyone in the near vicinity."

Laken looked at Joey, a question in her eyes.

"I don't have any experience," Joey said. "And frankly, I'm probably not a very good actress—"

"Ha!" Pacey scoffed. "She's just being modest. This is the luminous light who recently starred in the seminal art film, *Don and Dulcie.* It just got invited to the Sundance Film Festival."

"Really?" Laken asked, clearly impressed.

"Nah," Pacey admitted. "I just wanted to see if you'd buy it."

Laken laughed and wagged her finger at him. "Pacey," she said, "you are definitely in tomorrow night." She looked over at Joey again. "Were you really in such a movie, or was that part of the lie, too?"

"I was in it," Joey admitted. "But it was only some local thing."

"Made by perhaps the most talented not-yet-discovered filmmaker of this or any generation," Pacey intoned portentiously, "Mr. Dawson—"

Pacey didn't finish his statement. Because he had just noticed his best friend, the most talented not-yet-discovered filmmaker of this or any generation, enter the family room.

Hand in hand. With a girl.

A very cute girl.

Who was definitely not Joey Potter.

Chapter 6

Dawson looked down at his right hand, entwined with Patrice's. She had taken his hand right after they'd parked and gotten out of her car. And she hadn't let go since.

It's not that I don't want to hold her hand, Dawson thought. Actually, it's very nice. It's just that it feels so odd to be holding a hand other than Joey's. And it makes my hand feel like it belongs to someone else.

"At the risk of sounding like *The Real World*," Patrice began, "your ex, or, more correctly, your I'm-not-exactly-sure-what-you-are-anymore-although-you-still-care-deeply-and-always-will ex, is staring daggers at us."

Dawson whirled around, looking for Joey.

"There," Patrice nodded her chin. "Across the family room."

"Joey is definitely not staring daggers at us," Dawson corrected Patrice, his eyes still glued to Joey's face. "We're both seeing other people because we both want to see other people."

"You should see your expression," Patrice said. "Sort of preppie-esque panicked puppy."

Dawson tore his gaze away from Joey.

"You seem to be enjoying this little melodrama," Dawson said. "And I hate to have to disappoint you in your moment of vicarious angst, but Joey and I are completely fine about where our relationship is right now."

Patrice nodded solemnly. "Keep telling yourself that, Dawson. It would be delightful if at least one of us believed it, let alone both you and Joey."

Chris Wolfe came up behind Patrice, and playfully wrapped his long arms around her neck. "Patrice, Patrice, where have you been all my life?" he murmured huskily into her ear.

"Generally speaking, as far away from you as I could possibly get," Patrice said brightly. "Oh, thanks for inviting me to your party, by the way."

"No prob. Although I don't recall suggesting that you bring Dawson."

Patrice smiled sweetly. "Only because you harbored the hopeless fantasy of talking me out of my clothes and into your hot tub."

"Busted," Chris admitted, with a chuckle. "But that's all right, Patrice, I live for the chase another day." He clapped Dawson too heartily on the back. "You know I was just busting your chops, Dawson. I'm really glad you're here, man."

"Thanks, I think," Dawson replied. "Luckily for me, my innate sense of self was not tied up in whether or not you invited me to this party."

"For a movie you didn't get a gig on." Chris shook his head disgustedly. "What's up with that, man?"

"Lack of taste?" Dawson ventured.

Chris nodded in agreement. "Gotta be. You and I might have our differences at times, but you know more about film and are more talented than all the so-called professionals working on the movie put together."

"Well, I—" Dawson began.

"Yo, Chris, Linda's barfing in your hot tub!" someone standing by the sliding glass doors to the patio bellowed.

Chris cursed under his breath and took off.

"Well, there's your proof, Dawson. If Chris Wolfe says you're more talented than anyone working on the movie, then it's true. He never throws around compliments. And certainly not to you."

"I'm reasonably sure that the notches on Chris's bedpost are higher than his IQ," Dawson quipped, not wanting to let on how flattered he was by Chris's words.

"How wonderful to know that there will never be a notch named Patrice. Want to go out on the patio and dance? Assuming the wind is blowing the other way from the barfer in the hot tub?"

They headed out into the Indian summer night. The moon had risen over Chris's roof, casting a glow over the backyard. Out on the patio, as the music changed to a Lucinda Williams ballad, Dawson took Patrice into his arms.

Dancing next to them was Jen and a guy that Dawson thought he'd recognized from the crew, though with his faraway vantage point near the beach, he couldn't be certain.

"Hey, Dawson," Jen said, when she realized he was dancing next to her. "I'm surprised to see you here."

It was like a small wound in Dawson's pride. "I realize of course that this is a party for which I have no part," Dawson began defensively, "but Chris invited Patrice, and Patrice invited—"

"Dawson, take a breath," Jen interrupted him. "I meant surprised in a good way. As in, I'm glad you're here."

She nodded at the tall, dark-haired guy in whose arms she was swaying to the music. "This is Ken Latham. Ken's the A.D. on the picture. Ken, Patrice Reagen and my friend Dawson Leery. He's the one I told you about."

The song came to an end, and the four of them eased off the dance floor toward some empty lawn chairs.

"I'm not sure if I should be glad that my reputation preceded me or not," Dawson remarked, as he brushed some dirt and fallen leaves off a chair for Patrice.

"My hero," Patrice trilled comically, giving him a kiss on the cheek before she sat down.

"In this case, you can be glad," Ken told Dawson. "Jen says that you're a film genius."

At that moment, Dawson fell in love with Jen all over again.

"I told Ken what you told me about your interview with Arnie Bick," Jen confided, dropping her voice so that no one could overhear.

"What?" Patrice asked. She looked at Dawson. "You didn't tell me."

I don't know you well enough to have told you, Dawson thought, though he would never hurt her feelings by saying that aloud.

"It's . . . complicated," was what he actually said.

"Listen, I'm not one to bad-mouth people I work with," Ken said, "but this is my third film with the Arnster and he has a certain track record. When he's hiring locals, if anyone threatens his little fiefdom in any way, they never get the gig. I just wanted you to know that."

Dawson nodded gratefully. "Thank you for telling me. That's what I suspected. But it's nice to have it confirmed."

Patrice jumped up, her fists on her hips in a Supergirl pose. "Which one's Bick? I'll jack him up. And then I'll jack up his family."

They all laughed.

"I have a feeling I should have gotten to know you better a long time ago," Jen told Patrice.

"Oh, I'm just your usual run-of-the-mill girl who lives out her psychotic fantasies by drawing cartoons," Patrice said blithely. "The lead in the incredibly yawn-inducing, albeit apocryphal, youth theater play that gets trouped into every high school gym in America, *I'm Not Who You Think I Am.*"

"You ought to come hang out on the set," Ken said. "Great unintentional comic material for your cartoons."

"Yeah, like what?"

Ken puffed some air over his lower lip. "Actually, I have a big mouth, and just about now, I oughta be shutting it." He stood, and reached down for Jen's hand.

"Well, I have a big mouth, and nothing to lose," Jen said, as she got up, taking Ken's hand. "I know we've only been shooting for two days so far, but even I can see that the movie's in big trouble. Between Reginald London the Third and the Arnster—"

"Jen, Jen, my beautiful, darling, succulent assistant Jen!" Arnie Bick called, as he ran across the patio and practically vaulted himself at Jen.

"Down, boy," Jen said, moving out of his embrace.

Arnie laughed hysterically, his enormous Adam's apple bobbing in his skeletal neck.

"Jen, you sly foxette, you," Arnie chided her playfully. "I know how much you want me. And we're not on the job now, so . . ."

"Hey, Jen," Patrice said, "I forget—I know you told me when you're birthday is. Did you turn *sixteen* yet, or are you still *fifteen*? And what are the penalties in Massachusetts again for *sex with a minor*?"

Arnie paled. "Don't you know a joke when you hear one?" he asked Patrice. "Who are you, anyway?"

She put her fists on her hips, in Supergirl mode again. "Your worst nightmare, Arnie."

Arnie's head swiveled to Dawson, and recognition dawned in his eyes. "You! I recognize you. The swell-headed enfant terrible of small-town wherever I am."

"I have a name," Dawson said, through clenched teeth. "It's Dawson. Leery."

"Oh, thank you so much for reminding me," Arnie sniffed sarcastically. "Now I'll have to hire another hypnotist, to have it erased from my memory again." He turned to Ken.

"Ken, is there some reason you're hanging out with these children?"

"I happen to like these guys, Arnie," Ken said easily. "Say, I heard that there's a girl in the hot tub who's been looking for you. Some girl named Linda."

Arnie's eyes filled with lust. His Adam's apple took off toward the hot tub.

The rest of him followed.

"Is it him?"

"Is it really him?"

"Omigod, it is him, it has to be him!"

"I knew I should have worn a shorter skirt."

Suddenly, a buzz of excitement had come over everything female at Chris Wolfe's party. It was definitely not prompted by the arrival of the Arnster.

Pacey, who was free-feeding from the buffet table in the dining room, craned his neck to try to see what all the excitement was about. He turned to Joey, who was the only female in sight not hyperventilating.

"Can you please explain to me why this party just edged over the line into mass female psychosis?" Pacey asked. He grabbed a potato chip and popped it into his mouth.

Joey shrugged. "Some guy just came in. My guess is it's Burk Flint."

"Clearly, hoping for success beyond *Dripping Red*" Pacey quipped. "Am I supposed to know His Studliness?"

"For a guy who knows as much about thirty-year-old films as you do, Pacey, you are woefully uninformed about the latest heartthrob on the cover of various banal teen magazines."

Pacey, who had been busy erecting a towering cold cuts sandwich, lifted his creation to his mouth. "I'll take that as a compliment. Cheers." He bit.

"He starred in *Mega Hurts*, Pacey," Joey reminded him. "It was only the sleeper superficial-pretending-to-be-deep-teen-angst film of last year."

"Oh, well that explains it then," Pacey mumbled, his mouth full of sandwich. "I hate superficial sleepers pretending to be deep. Besides, as I recall, that was when I was busy being super-Pacey, with my super-girlfriend, and I, alas, missed out on many films."

"The film rated perhaps a C minus on my personal hit parade," Joey said. "However, I have to admit, Burk Flint rated a B, with a serious A potential."

Near the front door, the excited buzz escalated.

"Why look!" Pacey exclaimed. "Female pulchritude is parting, not unlike the Red Sea. Either this is an epic moment of biblical proportions, or the Flintstone cometh."

Burk Flint stepped through the parting crowd of admirers until at last Pacey could see him.

Tall. At least six one.

Chiseled. Like Scott Speedman playing the Rock of Gibraltar.

Sinewy muscle on top of sinewy muscle.

A way of walking that promised to elicit palpitations in all humans of the female persuasion.

"Now, you see Joey, here comes a walking example of why life is not fair. Even in my glory days as Pacey Buffman, I could not compete with that."

"No one could compete with that," Jen murmured, coming up behind him. She was by herself. "My IQ just bounced off the floor."

Dawson and Patrice edged their way through the crowd toward Jen and Pacey.

"Having fun?" Dawson asked them.

"More and more, all the time," Jen said, a half-smile on her face. She cocked her chin toward Burk. "Now, I ask you, is he hot, or is he hot?"

"He is, admittedly, one flavor-of-the-moment who looks even better in person than he did on film," Dawson mused. "However, great looking Hollywood flash-in-the-pans are a dime a dozen."

"Careful, Dawson, you're turning a little green," Pacey told him.

Dawson laughed derisively. "Pacey, surely you

know me better than to think I could possibly be jealous of a second-rate actor because he happens to have first-rate pectoral muscles?"

Pacey thought a moment. "Yeah, I guess you're right. I must have been thinking of myself. I gotta go pound some carbos."

He headed back to the food table, which gave Dawson a clear view of Joey standing nearby. Before he could even think about what to say, Patrice had taken the three steps over to Joey and stuck her hand out.

"Hi, Patrice Reagen."

Joey looked at her outstretched hand. "I know who you are," she said, not unkindly. "You were in my bio lab last year, right?" She shook Patrice's hand.

"I was the one drawing on the sketch pad instead of dissecting the dead frog," Patrice reminded her. "So, let me cut right to the chase. I'm out on a date with your ex. Do you have a problem with that?"

Dawson winced. He wished he could be just about anyplace other than where he actually was.

Joey pushed her hair off her face, and looped it behind her ear. "Why would I?" She reached for a cookie.

"Oh, I can think of lots of reasons," Patrice said. "Let's see, you want him back but you haven't told him yet. You don't want him back but it still makes you insane to see him with another girl. You might want him back but—"

"Excuse me, but since I am the subject of this excruciatingly embarrassing exchange, I would just like to say . . ."

Both girls waited, staring at him.

"Well?" Patrice asked.

The computer of Dawson's mind flipped through an assortment of conclusions to his sentence. Each worse than the one before.

"I would just like to say that . . ."

Mental computer crash.

"I'm going to . . . the bathroom. Excuse me."

Dawson turned purposefully on his heels and headed for the restroom off the kitchen.

And all he could think was: I just left Patrice Reagen and Joey Potter together. To bond. They have so much in common.

Art.

Me.

I am the biggest weenie in the world.

Chapter 7

"Jen, I changed my mind. I really do not think this is a good idea," Dawson told her.

It was two evenings later. He and Jen were standing on the corner of Main Street, a mere half block from the front door of Mondo Mocha, a new coffeehouse. Laken and her friends had easily talked the owners of Mondo Mocha into letting them do improv comedy there. It didn't hurt, of course, that most of them were actors from the movie.

In fact, the enterprising owner of the place had already placed a huge, homemade sign in the window:

APPEARING TONIGHT: IMPROV COMEDY
STARS OF *DRIPPING RED*

"C'mon, Dawson. Live dangerously." Jen took both his hands and started to pull him playfully toward Mondo Mocha.

"No, wait, I'm serious," Dawson insisted. "It was bad enough that I wasn't invited to Chris's party by anyone remotely connected to the movie. But now, to barge in on their improvisational comedy group—"

Jen groaned. "Let's do a quick reality check, shall we? We are going to *watch*. There is a big sign in the window practically begging people to come *watch*. This is not a private party, this is not by invitation only, this is you pay your two-dollar cover charge and you go in and have a Coke."

"I appreciate that, Jen, and I appreciate your introducing me to that assistant director, Ken—"

"Although I don't recall inviting that black cloud that's hanging over your head," Jen added. "Believe me, you should be glad you're not working on the movie. Because—how can I put this without hurting the Arnster's feelings?—his movie sucks. Hard."

"Why do I feel like someone is playing pinball in my intestines?" Pacey asked Laken, as he trod back and forth nervously across the tiny backstage area that had been draped off by the owner.

"Oh, that's perfectly normal," Laken assured him. "After all, we're going out there without any scripts, we take ideas from the audience, a lot of our attempts at humor will undoubtedly fail, and we'll make complete idiots out of ourselves in front of a packed house of strangers who paid their hard-earned money to see us."

"Was that supposed to cheer me up?" Pacey asked, incredulous.

"No. I just wanted to speed up your obligatory trip to the men's room so you'll be okay to go on stage in five minutes."

Pacey stared at her a moment, his face turning various hues of pale. "Excuse me!" he finally gasped, and sprinted for the john.

Laken turned to Joey, who was sitting on a folding chair behind her. "How come you look so calm?"

"I simply mask my terror better than he does," Joey admitted. "Right now, I'm trying to figure out why in the world I ever agreed to do this."

"Look at it this way: some people test themselves by jumping out of airplanes. But compared to going on stage to do improv comedy, they're wusses."

Burk Flint pushed open the side curtains and stepped backstage. "Hey guys, how goes it? Just wanted to tell you to break a leg." He kissed Laken on the cheek.

"You just feel bad because I get dripped to death by Red tomorrow," Laken replied, smiling. "You, meanwhile, get to live to the end of the film, get the girl, and get to be in *Dripping, II.*"

Joey shuddered. "You have to admit, a sequel is beyond frightening. And not in a good way."

Burk smiled at her. "Well, maybe the scene that Reginald decided today that you're gonna do with me will be your big break, Joey. You'll be such a big star by the time the sequel shoots, Arnie won't be able to afford you."

Flashing the two of them one last movie star smile, Burk waved good-bye and headed out into the audience. He spotted Jen, and headed for the table she was sharing with Dawson.

"Mind if I join you?" Burk asked.

"Please," Jen said, gesturing to an empty chair. She introduced Burk and Dawson to each other.

Burk contemplated Dawson. "I don't think I recognize you from the shoot. But then, I guess there are a lot of extras I haven't met."

It was everything Dawson could do to keep the steam from coming out of his ears.

"I'm not an extra," Dawson said tersely. "In fact, I'm not involved with the film. In any way. I'm a friend of Jen's."

Burk leaned across the table to Dawson. "Listen, between you and me, man, you're the luckiest guy in Capeside."

Dawson laughed. "I want you to know, I saw *Mega Hurts*. The movie lacked a certain cohesive vision, and the screenwriter didn't allow your character to develop very far, but I have to say, that given the limitations of the material, you were really quite good."

Burk looked both puzzled and amused, and scratched his head. "I'm not sure if you just complimented me or dissed the hell out of me."

"Knowing Dawson as I do," Jen said, "probably both. Dawson knows more about movies than Reginald will ever know. In fact, he should be working on the picture."

"So, why aren't you?" Burk asked Dawson.

Jen quickly explained Dawson's run-in with the Arnster. "Because of Arnie's ego, we don't get the benefit of Dawson's expertise."

Burk chuckled. "Okay, I'm not doubting that you might know a helluva lot more about movies than ol' Reggie," he began. "But neither of you seem to get the protocol of the movie biz. Because even if Dawson had a job on the movie, he'd be sharpening pencils or getting Kreamarino or kissing butt. And what he'd be doing best of all is keeping his mouth shut."

"But—" Jen began.

"Hey, that's just the way it is," Burk said with a shrug.

"Though I hate to admit it," Dawson said, "you're right."

Jen threw her hands in the air. "What is it with guys and their little . . . egos?" she fumed. "You're all so busy metaphorically playing mine-is-bigger-than-yours that—"

"Hi! I see you saved a seat for me."

Patrice Reagen slid into the fourth seat at their table.

For a moment, Dawson was taken aback.

Because he hadn't invited Patrice. Nor had he known that she was coming.

"Actually," Jen said, "that seat was for my friend Ken. He's coming to join us after he watches the dailies with Reginald and Arnie. But . . . I'll just pull up another chair." She reached for the only empty chair in sight, and slid it over.

Patrice leaned over and laced her fingers through Dawson's. "I overheard you and Jen at school saying that you were coming here. I wanted to surprise you, Dawson."

"Well, you did."

Patrice introduced herself to Burk, but she didn't have time to say anything more, as the houselights dimmed and the owner of Mondo Mocha took the stage.

"Hey everybody, great to see you here, what a crowd, huh?" said the barrel-chested, bearded owner of Mondo Mocha, into a microphone. "I really want to thank all the terrific people working on the film, both out of towners and locals, for coming out tonight to do and support our improv night."

He led the audience in applause.

"And now, put your hands together again—they told me they just named themselves backstage this minute—for the Drips!"

The small group of performers hustled onto the stage. Laken, Pacey, Joey, the second male lead—a boyish looking guy named Mark German, and Carrie Austin, who played the high school witch who gets dripped to death in the film's opening sequence, Lorell Courtlandt.

"Hi everybody, I'm Laken," Laken easily called to the audience. "As you know, actors should never make excuses for their work, and that's why I must tell you that we've had exactly one rehearsal, which was last night."

"So, we don't mind telling you," Mark went on,

"that we're really, really nervous. And that you should take pity on us. And even if we really suck, you should laugh really hard anyway."

That made the audience laugh.

"Excellent, just like that!" Laken exclaimed. "How improv works is, we'll be taking ideas from you, the audience, and coming up with—we hope—some really funny scenes, on the spur of the moment."

Laken quickly introduced everyone on stage. Joey was standing as far back on the stage as she could without falling off the edge, and Pacey looked shell-shocked.

Carrie stepped forward. "To open our show, we'd like to do our rendition of that classic rock hit "Clementine." Or, should I say, to the tune of "Clementine." Because our actual opening number is called . . . anybody? Somebody? A topic for the song?" She spread her hands to the audience.

"Hairballs!" someone called out instantly.

"Hairballs, gee, easy," Laken said dubiously. "So let me ask you a question, the lady who called out hairballs. What is it exactly that you have against us?"

The audience laughed again.

Patrice leaned toward Dawson. "I don't know who looks more freaked up there, Joey or Pacey."

"Me either."

Patrice kissed his cheek. "Did I mention that I missed you?"

Fortunately, Dawson didn't have time to answer

before Laken stepped forward to sing the first verse of "Hairballs," to the tune of "Clementine," to the accompaniment of Mark on the kazoo.

> *Oh my darling, it's alarming*
> *How hirsute you are below*
> *Hordes of flies they are all swarming*
> *'Cuz you put on such a show.*

The audience roared in laughter and applauded Laken's spur-of-the-moment cleverness.

Next, Carrie came forward and did a verse having to do with cats and their tendency to barf up their own fur. Joey fought her way through one about the fuzzy little balls on a sweater choking her to death. Finally, it was Pacey's turn.

He didn't step forward. He didn't move. He just stood there.

Mark gave him his kazoo introduction, as out in the audience Dawson winced in sympathy.

"Oh God," Jen said. "Poor Pacey."

Finally, at the last possible moment, Pacey lurched forward to the front of the stage. And then he sang:

> *Wiener schnitzel and a pretzel*
> *At the food court at the mall*
> *German tasties with some pastries*
> *Are the dinner of Herr Ball.*

The audience exploded into laughter and applause at the way Pacey used the German word

Herr, for "mister," and turned the improv in a completely different, hilarious direction.

And no one applauded harder than Jen and Dawson.

Forty-five minutes later—mostly funny with only a few duds—the lights came up for intermission. Ken had slipped into his seat a little while earlier.

"You missed the best improv of all," Jen told Ken. "Our friend Pacey was fabulous." She peered at him. "And might I add, you do not look like a man enjoying an evening of comedy. Your clenched jaw is a quick giveaway."

Ken sighed. "I didn't come here to rain on your parade, so just forget it. Hey Burk, havin' fun?"

"Not now that I got a look at your face," Burk said.

"I bet it's the dailies," Patrice guessed. "I love throwing around showbiz terms. It's so . . . showbiz."

Dawson looked at her. "How do you know what dailies are?"

"Well, I know that film is your love. And I believe that when you really care about someone, you should learn all about what they love. So I took a few books out of the library, and read them. Cover to cover."

Dawson tried to smile in appreciation at her, but his mouth didn't seem to be working correctly.

She's such a nice girl, Dawson thought guiltily.

*And she's really pretty. And nice. And into me. So
do I wish she would just spontaneously combust?*

Jen caught herself looking askance at Patrice, but
quickly looked away.

"Hey, your problems with the dailies are my problems with the dailies, Ken," Burk said, his voice
concerned. "What was wrong?"

"You sure you want to hear this?" Ken asked,
hesitating.

"Well, I'm sure," Jen said. "It's bad enough they
don't let Kreamarino girl into the dailies. So, spill
your guts."

"You know the opening killing," Ken began
slowly, "where Lorell gets dripped to death in her
bedroom? Well, she's supposed to be this total
witch, right? And the audience is supposed to be
glad, in a way, to see her get offed. Except it happens so early on there's no character development
yet. So we don't care about Lorell one way or the
other. The scene just doesn't work."

"Yeah, I see the problem," Burk said.

"Okay, stop me if I don't know what I'm talking
about," Jen began. "But couldn't they just put the
scene in later? Change the order of things? And add
a scene earlier where we get to see what a witch she
is?"

Ken shook his head. "Doubtful. Budget."

"I could offer some assistance, unless I'm step-
ping on toes . . ." Dawson said hesitantly.

"Go ahead, man, at this point I'll take all the help
I can get—unlike certain people who shall go
nameless," Ken encouraged.

Dawson tapped one finger contemplatively against his lips. "You can say a lot with very little, actually. First of all, you can set her up visually. For example, the screen saver on her computer monitor might be a working guillotine with Laken's character's head in it. She's a big root-for, right?"

"Right!" Patrice exclaimed enthusiastically, which seemed odd, since as far as Dawson knew, she had never seen the script for the movie.

"And then," Dawson went on, "Lorell might have a poster from *Jawbreaker* on her wall. And before she gets into bed, she kisses Rose McGowan's picture and says something like, 'You're my goddess.' "

"Oh my God," Patrice cried. "Is that brilliance, or what?"

"No, frankly, it isn't," Dawson said, embarrassed at her enthusiasm.

Ken thought a moment. "You know, Dawson, that might actually work."

"And it would be cheap to shoot, right?" Jen added. "Even Arnie can't object."

"It's a hell of a lot better than anything in the script," Burk chimed in.

Ken nodded, looking at Dawson with admiration. "Thanks. There's only one problem."

"What's that?" Dawson asked.

"If I tell Reginald and Arnie that the idea came from you, Dawson, they'll decide it's the worst idea in the history of motion pictures."

"That's true," Jen agreed reluctantly.

"So, what do you want me to do?" Ken asked. "It's your call."

"Frankly, from my point of view, there's no downside," Dawson told him. "If you're asking me if I mind giving the idea and not getting credit for it, the answer is no, I don't mind."

Jen's eyebrows shot skyward. "Dawson, selflessness in love is one thing. But I have never known you to be selfless in matters of art."

Patrice shook her head. "Well, maybe you just don't know my Dawson as well as you think you do." Her hand covered Dawson's, and she smiled beatifically.

Dawson was speechless. What could he possibly say? But he'd have to deal with Patrice later, though he had no idea how.

"Take the idea, Ken," Dawson offered, "with my compliments. Frankly, as artistic ideas go, it's rather puny."

"All right, then, thanks. You've done your good deed for the year," Ken told him.

"You're a hell of a guy, Dawson," Burk said, with admiration. "But then, I had already heard that from Jen. And a couple of other buds of yours on the film."

"So, always nice to know that my friends are saying complimentary things about me, behind my back," Dawson said, feigning an ease he was no longer feeling. "And who were they, by the way?"

"You know, the two friends of yours in the Drips. Pacey—that guy's a riot. And Joey. She's really terrific, by the way."

"You think so?" Dawson asked, annoyed.

"Oh yeah. And I'm not the only one who thinks so. Reginald makes a lot of dumb decisions, but even he sees Joey's po. That's why he's putting her in this beach scene we're shooting tomorrow."

"Oh?" Dawson asked.

"As my girlfriend."

Chapter 8

"Thanks for getting up so early to have breakfast with me, Jack," Joey said. "I really appreciate it." She swallowed a bit of pancake.

"Hey, what are ex-boyfriends for? Besides, it's a delightful in-service day, and there's no school."

It was the next morning, and the two of them were sitting in a booth at the back of the Mollye's Coffee Shop. Joey had to be on the set at eight o'clock, so she'd asked Jack to meet her for breakfast at seven.

She was sure he'd say no, but, to her surprise, he agreed. And, even though Arnie Bick provided coffee and doughnuts at the catering truck, the place was jammed. Clearly, too many people had already gotten sick of eating too many of Arnie's stale doughnuts, and consuming too much of his Kreamarino-laced instant coffee.

He kept the brewed stuff in his private trailer.

"I kind of wanted to ask your advice about something," Joey told him.

"Well, that's flattering. Personally, I would nominate myself as the guy in Capeside least likely to give good advice, seeing as how I've mucked up my own life so badly. But I'll give it a shot."

Joey shot him a dubious look. "That doesn't exactly fill me with confidence, Jack. Besides, as usual, you're being way too hard on yourself."

She reached for her orange juice and took a swallow.

"Ah, the old orange juice delay tactic," Jack noted.

Joey set down the glass. "It's about Dawson."

"Color me shocked."

"Very funny. I mean, it's only secondarily about Dawson, actually," Joey told him, and quickly explained to him that day's shooting; that she'd be in a scene where she'd be playing Burk's girlfriend.

"And that has something to do with Dawson because—?"

"I told you, it was secondarily," Joey defended herself. "Last night, before I left Mondo Mocha, Dawson asked me if it was true that I would be playing a love scene with Burk."

"Yes?"

"And he asked in that typical Dawson way, where he pretends simply to be eliciting information, when, in fact, it seemed to bother him."

"Well, that's Dawson all right," Jack agreed. "And it's also not your problem."

"I know that. And whatever Dawson might think about whatever choices I make right now, it doesn't affect me one way or the other," Joey concluded.

"So I guess that means you invited me to breakfast because you missed me desperately," Jack surmised, a twinkle in his eye.

Joey balled up her napkin and tossed it on her plate in disgust. "I tell myself that I don't care what Dawson thinks, or what Dawson does. What I need to know is that Dawson and I have mutually agreed that it's over."

Jack grinned at her. "I bet Dawson would know."

"Just for that, you're buying breakfast."

"Deal. But I'm assuming you're getting extra bucks for your big scene with the star. So after you get paid, you can take me out for dinner."

Jack put some money on the table, and they slipped out of the booth.

"You didn't say anything about how you feel about doing this scene with Burk," Jack pointed out, as he held the door to Main Street open for Joey.

"Like you said, I like the extra money."

"And that's it?" Jack queried. "You get picked out of all of the extras to do some big love scene with the star—"

"Let's not exaggerate, Jack. I have all of two lines. And then he goes back to his real girlfriend, who is the star of the movie."

"Whatever. It's still a big deal. And all you can say is, 'I like the extra money'?"

Joey shrugged, slipping on her sunglasses. "Sure."

Jack thought a moment. "I know that patented

Joey shrug all too well, and that shrug generally means the opposite of what it is intended to convey."

"I believe my next line is, I have no idea what you're talking about."

"Wow. That means it's worse than I thought," Jack said.

"Irritation is starting to erode my sunny mood."

"Because you know I'm right. It's written all over your face, Joey. This isn't really about Dawson at all. It's about Burk. You're into him. Really into him. And now that you have to do a love scene with him, you don't know what the hell to do about it."

Against her better judgment, Jen reached for a stale doughnut from the service tray, and poured herself a cup of instant sock juice. It was ten in the morning, and Reginald had not yet begun to shoot the scene of Joey and Burk together on the beach, which had been scheduled to begin two hours earlier. The powers that be were still holed up in Reginald's trailer, arguing about the movie.

Arnie had actually stuck his head out once, and asked her to bring her his usual Kreamerino'd coffee, and when she'd brought it into the trailer, Ken had made brief eye contact with her.

His face said it all. Things were not going well.

That had been over an hour ago. And they were still on hold.

As Jen bit into the stale doughnut, her eyes wandered to the roped-off area at the end of the beach, where she saw Dawson standing.

Thinking twice about her culinary choice—even a growling stomach was better than that—she flung the doughnut to a flock of terns and strode over to Dawson.

"And what brings you to the other side of the rope this fine morning?" she asked him.

"Just observing," Dawson observed.

"Observing nothing," Jen replied. "We haven't shot an inch of film today."

"Imagine. A low-budget film with very little to do, and yet the director still manages to be behind schedule and over budget."

Jen couldn't help noticing that Dawson's eyes were focused beyond her, on the small portable tent that had been erected in the sand about a hundred feet away. In the shade of the tent, Burk and Joey sat on canvas chairs, waiting to be called to action.

"Welcome to J.A.," Jen said. She turned her head to look at Joey, and then back at Dawson. "Joey Anonymous. Hi, my name is Dawson, and I'm a Joey-aholic. Hi, Dawson!"

Dawson gave her a cool look. "I presume that was meant to amuse."

"Funny, I find me hilarious. Besides, the addict is always the last one to find humor in his own addiction."

"Jen, I am not addicted to Joey," Dawson insisted. "But what kind of friend would I be if I simply stopped caring about her just because she and I are no longer romantically involved?"

Jen pulled a stick of gum from the back pocket of

her overalls and unwrapped it. "I know I've already seen this movie, Dawson, because I recognize that line. Want gum?"

Dawson shook his head. "It isn't a movie, and you know it. Contrary to what you may think, Jen, I do not confuse movies with real life."

Jen popped the stick of gum into her mouth. "Uh-huh."

"Isn't Joey supposed to shoot her scene with Burk this morning?" Dawson asked.

"Yeah, like you don't know," Jen said, laughing.

"What exactly does it entail, if you don't mind my asking?"

She reached into the back pocket of her overalls and pulled out a dog-eared copy of the movie script. She handed it to Dawson.

"Read it and weep. Or, should I say, drip. Page sixteen."

Dawson thumbed through the script, until he reached the scene where, after Burk's character, Tom, had temporarily broken up with his girlfriend, he was on a date to the beach bonfire with a new girl named Ashleigh.

"Ashleigh is sexy in a natural way," the script said. "She wears a tiny bathing suit and it's clear that she's crazy about Tom."

Dawson looked up at Jen. "A tiny bathing suit? What exactly does that mean?"

Jen chewed her gum. "It means, Dawson, small."

"Small as in two piece as opposed to one piece? Bikini as opposed to two piece? Thong as opposed to—"

"Why don't you just wait and see when Joey pulls off that white terrycloth beach robe, Dawson. I seem to recall that Reginald rewrote his copy so that she's nude."

For a brief instant, Dawson's face paled. Then, he realized that Jen was making a joke. At his expense.

"I just hate to see Joey being exploited in some cheap cheesy film, that's all," Dawson said. "And how could they be shooting this scene now, anyway? It's supposed to be a bonfire party on the beach. At *night*."

"Change of plans," Jen explained. "There are too many scenes after dark, and not enough time to shoot them all. So their little love scene got changed to the two of them playing hooky and going to a deserted strip of beach. During the day."

"Gee, how wildly creative," Dawson said sarcastically.

"Yeah, that Reginald, he's a genius."

"Oh, great," Dawson groaned. "Joey just looked over here and saw me. She's going to think I was spying on her."

"Well, you were."

"That is completely untrue, Jen. Besides, I'm leaving now. It just so happens that I've started work on a new film script, and—"

"Hi!"

Patrice ran over to Dawson and Jen, her sketch pad under her arm. "What a coincidence! I was up the beach drawing my latest cartoon strip and I saw you guys."

"What a coincidence," Jen echoed dubiously.

"It is so totally not right that you are on *this* side of *that* rope, Dawson," Patrice said.

"I'll second that," Jen agreed. "But I'm sure whatever your latest opus is, Dawson, it's much better than *Dripping Red,* anyway."

"You're writing a new movie?" Patrice asked, beyond excited. "When can I read it?"

"When it's done would probably be a good time," Dawson replied. He disliked himself for the nasty edge to his voice. And yet, he couldn't help himself. Every time Patrice showed up, uninvited and unexpected, it made him irritable.

And he just couldn't figure out *why.*

"I totally understand that you wouldn't want anyone to read it until you're done," Patrice assured Dawson. "After all—"

"People! People!"

Patrice was interrupted as Arnie's voice rang through the bullhorn. "We're behind schedule, and we have a lot of catching up to do, so chop-chop!" He handed the bullhorn to the nearest flunky, and looked around until he saw Jen. He crooked a finger at her, and motioned like he was drinking coffee.

Jen groaned. "Excuse me. Kreamarino beckons. Catch you guys later."

She hurried toward Arnie's trailer.

"Isn't there some kind of union or feminist organization she can complain to?" Patrice asked. "I mean, she didn't sign up for that job so she could make his stupid coffee!"

"I totally agree with you," Dawson said. "Jen is

85

probably smarter, and definitely more talented, than Arnie will ever be."

Patrice flipped open her sketch pad to a blank page, and took a razor-fine black pen from her back pocket. Then she quickly drew a large circle with a tiny circle above it and a tiny circle below it. And below the bottom tiny circle she drew two little stick legs, with little feet. Then, over the character's tiny head, she drew a bubble. And inside the bubble she wrote "Kreamarino! And don't skimp!"

She held the sketch pad out to Dawson. "Guess who?"

Dawson laughed as Patrice scrawled, "Arnie Taking His Adam's Apple Out for a Walk" under the cartoon.

It's so strange, Dawson thought. *One minute I wish Patrice would just get out of my sight forever. And the next minute I think she's the absolute greatest girl I've met in a really long time.*

"So, you want to stay and watch Joey's unveiling, or do you want to go get an early lunch?" Patrice asked.

Before Dawson could answer, he saw Joey stand up, take off her robe, and hand it to a gofer.

He gulped uneasily.

He'd just discovered how tiny "tiny" could be.

Chapter 9

Joey stared down at her teensy-weensy pink bikini bottom and tried in vain to pull its material, so that more of her skin would be covered.

Hopeless.

"Maybe we could try a different bathing suit," she told Diane, who was in charge of wardrobe.

"Yeah, and maybe I could get fired. But I'm not going to," Diane replied. "Reginald picked this bathing suit out for you personally."

"Why doesn't that make me feel any better?"

Burk, who had been called away for a moment, strode back over to the tent where Joey was standing. It was the first time he had seen her without her robe.

"You look great in that," he told her easily.

"Actually, what I look is almost naked. And what

I feel is almost foolish. Which almost makes me wish I hadn't said yes to this, except that I more than almost need the money." She sighed, and tried to pull the top of the bikini up, in an effort to cover more of her breasts.

It was equally hopeless.

"Quiet on the set!" a flunky cried. "Girls jogging on the beach, take one."

"And . . . action!" Ken said.

Three extremely busty girls began to jog along the shoreline, while Reginald filmed.

"More sprightly, girls!" Reginald called. "More enthusiasm! You're young, you're happy, you're free. I need more bounce!"

The girls dutifully began to lift their knees higher as they ran.

Jen sidled over to Joey, her eyes on the trio of joggers. "Look at it this way, Joey," Jen said. "It could be worse."

"How?"

"That could be you."

"Fantastic, girls!" Reginald called. "I adore you. I want you to bear my children. I want you to do it again!"

"Working on this movie ought to come complete with a hurl sack," Jen muttered. "And to think, I was so excited about working on my first professional film. Compared to this dreck, Dawson's earliest efforts ranked with Louis Malle."

"Oh, Jen, honey-sweetie-baby-cookie," Arnie called to her from outside his trailer. "I'm in intense need of your services."

"That does it." Jen turned and marched over to Arnie. "Look, Mr. Bick—"

"Jen, Jen, Jen, have you considered therapy? You really have a lot of hang-ups about intimacy, for one so young. For example, you've gone back to calling me by my last name."

"Mr. Bick," Jen repeated, quite deliberately, "you hired me to be your assistant. I was under the impression that the assistant to the assistant producer of a movie would have duties that actually involved something to do with the making of that movie. But so far, I have fetched forty-seven cups of Kreamarino'd coffee for you, fended off your wandering hands, and come running every time you called my name. But I draw the line at having you scream out that you are *in need of my services!*"

Arnie pulled a money clip from his pants pocket and extracted several bills. "I totally grok. *Stranger in a Strange Land*. My favorite book. I've been trying to get the rights for years—"

"Did you have a point, Arnie?" Jen fumed.

"Absolutely. You have a lot of po, Jen. And I hate to see so many hang-ups in one so young. But I know how expensive therapy can be. So what say I spot you a few hundred, you go to one of those Esalen-type specialists who help you get in touch with your inner child—"

"Excuse me, Arnie?" Jen interrupted.

"Yes?"

"It's not that I wasn't hanging on every word. And I wouldn't interrupt unless it was deathly important. But I—"

She had been about to utter the word "quit," when she was stopped by Reginald's running over to them and throwing his arms around her and Arnie simultaneously.

"I am so happy, I could weep," Reginald gushed.

"That's wonderful news, Reggie," Arnie replied. "And what, may I ask, is the cause of your joy?"

"I believe I've figured out how to fix the scene with Lorell," Reginald said. "I'm going to establish her bitchiness *visually*. It was a stroke of genius, really—"

Ken had joined them in time to overhear what Reginald was saying.

"And I must give some of the credit to my wonderful A.D.," Reginald added magnaminously. He beckoned with his hand for Ken to join in the group hug, a gesture that Ken managed to ignore.

"You're my new muse, Mr. Kenneth," Reginald said playfully. "Ask a favor of me. Any favor. Arnie's in the kind of mood where he might actually say yes." Reginald poked Arnie playfully in the ribs.

"Actually, there is something you could do for me," Ken said.

"Just name it, my boy," Reginald insisted.

"Well, I know that Daphne—she's one of the gofers—is really dying to be Arnold's assistant. And I've noticed that Jen has an excellent eye. So, I was wondering . . . if Jen might become the assistant to the A.D.?"

"No can do, man," Arnie said. "Jen here is indispensible to me."

Reginald looked thoughtful. "And which one is Daphne again?"

Ken looked around, until his eyes lit on a statuesque blond in a very tight T-shirt that bared her very tanned abs, and a shiny metal navel ring. "Her."

"On second thought, I might be able to do without Jen," Arnie said quickly, a gleam of lust in his eye.

He hurried away toward the girl. "Oh. Daphne!" he called. "I have the most wonderful news for you!"

Reginald smiled at Ken and Jen. "There. I like my people to be happy."

"And you've just made your people very happy," Jen said. "Thank you."

"Excellent." Reginald turned to Ken. "And now, it's time to finally get that lust-filled scene of Tom and Ashleigh on the beach."

"Just slip into the double sleeping bag, darlings," Reginald instructed Burk and Joey.

Joey looked at him uncertainly. "But, uh, this was supposed to be a nighttime scene?"

"I've changed my vision," Reginald told her. "The two of you came out here last night, to be alone. You finally got a chance at the boy you've always loved, Ashleigh. And vixen that you are, you took it. And him."

"But . . . my first line is supposed to be, 'Tom, look at the stars. They're so beautiful.' "

"And then I say," Burke said, " 'Almost as beautiful as you are, Ashleigh.' "

"Yes, yes, I'm familiar with the script," Reginald said testily. "I'm making a few changes. Now, Ashleigh, you just finished spending a torrid night in Tom's arms. You've stolen him from your best friend—"

"But how can I be her best friend, when you never see me in any other scenes in the movie?" Joey asked, truly baffled.

"You've been *away at boarding school*," Reginald instructed, with growing irritation. "Now then. After your torrid night of love, you've slept nearly 'til noon. The sun is high in the sky, when you awaken. And you look at the boy you so callously stole. And you say, 'Tom, look at the waves. They're so beautiful.' "

Joey didn't know whether to laugh or cry. But she was pretty sure either response would have her thrown off the movie set. And she really did need the money.

So she took her cue from Burk, who was nodding thoughtfully.

She did the same.

"And then, Burk—Tom, your line is the same. And then, Ashleigh, your final line is, 'You're all mine, now, Tom. I could just eat you up.' "

Joey just stared at him. "You're kidding."

It was clear from the look on the director's face that he was not at all kidding.

Plus, Burk was nodding thoughtfully again.

Reginald clapped his hands together briskly. "All right, my beautiful bunnies, let's hop, hop, hop into that sleeping bag." He nodded to Ken. "I believe you can take it from here. I need perspective."

With that, Reginald walked away.

"Okay, you heard what the man said," Ken told his crew, and then turned to Jen. "Can you please make sure Joey is in the sleeping bag facing camera number two? And Burk should be on his back, with his arms behind his head, as if he's asleep."

"No time like the present," Jen told Joey and Burk, gesturing toward the double sleeping bag. "You guys get in, and let the hair and makeup people touch you up before we shoot."

As soon as Joey and Burk got into the bag, two young women descended on them, with portable makeup and hair kits. The brunette pulled down the straps of Joey's bikini top, and began to apply a thick greasy pancake makeup to Joey's shoulders and chest.

"Hey, what's that for?" Joey protested.

"You can just take the top off, if you want to," the makeup woman said. "Frankly, you'd make my life a lot easier that way."

Joey pushed the woman's arm away. "As much as I'd love to make your life easier, you still didn't answer my question."

"You're supposed to be naked in the scene," the woman told her, as if that were the most obvious thing in the world. "Hello? Who seduces a guy on the beach and wakes up with her bathing suit on?"

"Me," Joey said firmly. "Ashleigh is much more shy than you thought."

"I think I can help," Burk said. "if you don't mind."

Joey looked at him warily, and shrugged.

"Look, if you just let her put the pancake makeup on your neck and shoulders, down to your cleavage, then it'll match your face. You can still have your top on, with the straps lowered. And we'll just make sure the sleeping bag doesn't go lower than *here*," Burk told her, making a gesture just below his collarbone.

Jen nodded her agreement, but Joey asked her to check with Ken to make sure that no one expected her to show body parts that she had no intention of showing.

Ken confirmed. So Joey did it.

Nodding thoughtfully, of course.

"Look at that!" Dawson exclaimed, pointing toward Joey and Burk in the sleeping bag. "It looks like she's completely naked."

"Well, that's the whole point, Dawson," Patrice said. "They're supposed to have just done it all night. Did you think she'd be wearing sweats?"

She wore them often enough when she slept with me, Dawson thought. But then, we never did it all night. In fact, we never did it at all. In fact—

He put his hands over his ears, as if that gesture would stop the tape in his head.

He'd been dealing with the Joey thing so well, too. And now . . . well now, he was torturing himself anew. Because as much as he told himself that he should have taken Patrice up on her offer to go to an early lunch, and stop watching Joey, he just hadn't been able to do it.

Now, Joey was in a double sleeping bag with Burk Flint, who clearly registered a twelve on a girl-bait scale of ten, with the straps of her bikini top pulled down so low that she looked like she was naked.

And, on top of that, she looked happy about the situation.

"Listen, you think that I don't know how you feel, but I do," Patrice said. "This one time, at art camp, this guy who had been my boyfriend like forever, broke up with me, and started going out with this really gorgeous girl who worked with Clay."

With his attention still focused on Joey, Dawson asked, "What did she do? Throw clay pots?"

"No. The guy's name was Clay Hepbern, actually. And I don't think she could have thrown him. 'Cuz he weighed like two hundred pounds." Patrice put her hand on Dawson's arm. "You need to be distracted."

Barely listening, Dawson muttered "Uh-huh." Joey was snuggling closer to Burk.

Now Patrice swung Dawson around, so he was facing her, grabbed him by the T-shirt, and kissed him.

Dawson was so shocked all he could do was stand there.

When Patrice pulled away, she was grinning at him.

"Well?"

"That was . . . completely unexpected," Dawson managed.

"You could use a little more of the unexpected in your life, Dawson," Patrice observed.

He took one last look at Joey, who was now rapt in Burk's overdeveloped arms. "You may actually be right, Patrice." He forced himself to turn away from the sight on the beach that was torturing him, and put out his hand.

Beaming with happiness, Patrice took it.

Hand in hand, they walked away.

Chapter 10

Dawson lay on his bed, watching the final frames of *Splendor in the Grass* on his VCR. Funny how Natalie Wood always reminded him of Joey. And funny how he found himself renting old Natalie Wood movies.

The low point had come the evening before, when he'd watched *Miracle on Thirty-fourth Street* back-to-back with *Inside Daisy Clover.*

Inside Daisy Clover was a truly horrible film. But when teen Natalie Wood was singing as Daisy, it was Joey's face that Dawson saw on the screen. When Natalie was laughing, when she was crying, when she was kissing Robert Redford, in Dawson's mind it was Joey.

Now, on the TV screen, Natalie Wood drove away from Warren Beatty's house while her voiceover recited lines from the famous Walt Whitman poem: "And nothing can bring back of the hour of splendor in the grass . . ."

Dawson closed his eyes, sighed, and rolled over onto his stomach. He hadn't seen any of his friends in three days. They were all busy working on the movie. Which left him more than enough time to think about Joey and Burk in the sleeping bag.

Burk, his arms around Joey, pulling Joey to his manly chest.

He knew it wasn't fair—after all, he and Joey could have been together if he had taken her up on her offer. But he knew it wasn't right.

Even so, he didn't like the idea of Joey taking up the same kind of offer from Burk.

Rrrr-ing!

Dawson's phone. He contemplated not answering it, the better to wallow in his own misery.

But after the fourth ring, he snatched it off his nightstand.

"Hello?"

"You're wallowing, aren't you?" Pacey accused him, through the phone.

"I'm studying some old movies, actually," Dawson replied defensively.

"How many of these movies star Natalie Wood?"

Dawson was silent.

"I knew it," Pacey crowed. "Besides, I'm next door at Jen's and we felt your ennui all the way over here. That's a scary thing, Dawson."

"Ah, the Andie McPhee influence," Dawson parried. "Andie is the only girl I know who actually uses the word *ennui* in a spoken sentence."

"Yeah, you gotta love her vocabulary building skills—and don't change the subject. And now, Dawson, I suggest you hang up the phone. You are about to get company. You know how rude it is to be gabbing on the phone when your buds show up."

The phone went dead in Dawson's ear. Which gave him no opportunity to say what he would have said:

I don't feel like company. I want to be alone.

Etcetera, etcetera.

Moments later, Dawson heard noise downstairs, then footsteps thundering up to his room. Laughing hysterically, Jen, Pacey, and Laken pushed into his room. Jen scrambled onto Dawson's bed and jumped up and down like a little kid.

"Jen, while I'm sure you weigh next to nothing," Dawson began, "I doubt that my parents would appreciate your wrecking the box springs."

She fell onto her butt. "Oh come on, Dawson, you're starting to look way too tragic hero—esque. Snap out of it!"

Dawson stepped further away from the bed. "While I appreciate your exuberance, I'm sorry that I don't share the same frame of mind."

"It's a little known fact that exuberance is catchy," Laken said, grinning. "We're celebrating. I got dripped to death today. And the Drips are performing at Mondo Mocha in exactly two hours."

"The really big news of the evening," Pacey

chimed in, "is that the Drips are adding a new Drip this evening. In fact, consensus is that he is undoubtedly the biggest drip of all."

Dawson took in their faces.

And it dawned on him who they were talking about.

"You do realize there's absolutely no way I'm getting on stage to do improvisational comedy," Dawson told them.

"Wrong," Jen sang out. "Come on, Dawson. It'll be fun and you know it."

Dawson shook his head. "Watching last time was fun. But participating this time would be—"

"Even more fun!" Laken concluded.

Dawson shook his head vehemently. "Thanks, but no thanks."

Pacey sighed dramatically, and looked at Laken.

"In order to get Dawson to do what he really wants to do, but doesn't realize that he really wants to do, one has to be familiar with the skewered psychological profile that is Dawson Leery. To wit: the subtle use of reverse psychology."

Pacey walked over to Dawson and wrapped one arm around his friend's shoulders. "I understand that you suffer from severe performance anxiety, and that you're secretly afraid that I will be infinitely more clever than you on stage, thus shrinking what little ego-strength you have left."

Dawson shot Pacey a jaded look. "Frankly, Pacey, that was a pathetic effort."

"So then, it wouldn't bother you if I outshone you on stage?" Pacey asked innocently.

"Of course not," Dawson replied.

Pacey nodded. "And it wouldn't bother you to share a stage with Joey?"

"Pacey, this is—" Dawson began.

Pacey ignored him. "And it wouldn't bother you to know that Burk-my-abs-are-made-of-granite-Flint plans to come ogle the object of your massive wallowing *ce soir*, either?"

Dawson turned to Jen. "Has it escaped your attention that where Pacey was formerly merely irritating, he has now escalated to the point of insufferable?"

"You can try to shift everyone's focus to me all you want, Dawson," Pacey said breezily. "None of us are fooled. Basically, you feel like crap. And basically—"

"Hel-lo!" a voice called from downstairs. "Anyone home?"

Dawson groaned, and closed his eyes.

Patrice.

Why did she always seem to find the perfectly wrong time to show up?

He hadn't seen her since they'd had lunch three days earlier, even though she had called him twice and left messages on his answering machine.

He hadn't called her back.

Now he could see that he was about to pay the price.

"Excuse me," he told his friends. Bowing to the inevitable, Dawson started to go downstairs to invite Patrice up. "Patrice, I'll be right there!"

"You sly dog, you," Jen called after Dawson. "You

didn't want to come with us because you have a date with Patrice."

Dawson stopped to explain, but was cut off when Patrice rushed happily into his room.

What drove Dawson really crazy was that she looked so cute. There she was, a darling girl, smart, funny, talented, and beaming at him the way the rest of the females in Capeside were beaming at Burk Flint.

Which means I should be glad to see her, Dawson thought. *So why aren't I?*

"Hey, what's up?" Patrice went over to Dawson and gave him a big hug.

"Not much," Dawson replied. It felt ridiculous to have Jen and Pacey grinning knowingly at them. Clearly, they thought he and Patrice were a couple. Protesting to the contrary was, at the moment, out of the question.

"So, Dawson, let's go do something fun," Patrice suggested, still hanging on him.

"Gee, I'd really like to," Dawson lied, thinking fast. "But I already promised . . . Pacey I'd go do something with him."

Patrice finally removed her arms from Dawson's neck. "Oh," she uttered softly, clearly disappointed. "Well, I was just in the neighborhood, so I thought . . ."

She let the rest of her sentence hang in the air.

Dawson took in her embarrassed and disappointed face.

At this moment, I dislike myself as much as Patrice seems to like me, Dawson said to himself.

Patrice moved self-consciously toward the door. "Okay, well, I'll just be going then. Talk to you soon, Dawson."

She disappeared downstairs.

For a long moment, no one spoke.

"I believe this is known as your basic pregnant pause," Jen finally said.

Pacey shook his head, baffled. "Correct me if I'm wrong, Dawson. Didn't you just blow off a really hot girl who, misguided as she may be, seems to be crazy about you?"

Dawson grabbed his jacket. "Let's just go do improv."

"All I have to say is, that was a whole lotta drama just to get the guy to come do some improv comedy with us," Laken said.

And, as they hurried downstairs, she added, "Can someone please explain to me what that was all about?"

No one could.

Once Dawson got to Mondo Mocha, he changed his mind again. So his friends went backstage to prepare without him, leaving Dawson alone at a table to nurse a Coke.

Pacey was sure it was some kind of competitive thing, and Dawson wasn't sure Pacey was entirely wrong.

But mostly, it was as if his friends had made a new circle, and he wasn't inside it. Instead he was outside somewhere with Patrice. The whole thing depressed him so much that he felt certain that, were he to go on stage with the Drips, he'd be more likely to make people cry than laugh.

He took a sip of his Coke and reached for a handful of popcorn from the bowl in the middle of the table just as Jack arrived.

"Hey, Dawson," Jack said, sliding into the chair opposite him. "What happened? Jen told me she and Pacey were planning to get you up there with them tonight."

"They did their best," Dawson said. "I think I'm better off as a behind-the-scenes kind of artist."

Jack nodded. "In other words, you chickened out."

"Why does everyone act as if my doing improv comedy is akin to the car racing chickie run scene in *Rebel Without a Cause*?" Dawson asked.

Then he winced at his own question.

Because *Rebel Without a Cause* featured, in addition to James Dean, none other than Natalie Wood.

"Talked to Joey lately?" Dawson asked Jack.

Jack scratched his chin. "Yeah, just about every day."

Even though it was ridiculous under the circumstances—Dawson felt the old heat of competitiveness with Jack over Joey creep up the back of his neck.

Because it wasn't like *he* was talking to Joey every day.

Stop it, he told himself. I mean, Jack is gay, for crying out loud.

Dawson checked his watch. Five minutes to show time.

"I want you to know, Jack, that I'm really glad Joey has a friend like you," Dawson said.

Jack's eyebrows went up. "Meaning what? One who's light in his loafers?"

Dawson flushed. "No, no, you totally misunderstand me. My comment had nothing at all to do with your sexual orientation."

"Or disorientation, as the case may be," Jack added dryly.

"What I mean is," Dawson hurried on, "a friend who really cares about her, who has her best interests at heart." He reached for another handful of popcorn. "And I'm sure as her friend—and as my friend, and knowing that I care about her as I do—as a friend, I mean—that if anything negative or troubling were going on in Joey's life, you'd probably share that with me."

Jack looked noncommittal.

"Right?" Dawson asked.

"Probably not," Jack admitted. "I know you like to think of yourself as her knight in shining armor, Dawson. But the truth of the matter is, if she wants you to know something, she'll tell you herself."

Agony.

Because Dawson knew he had been replaced not only as her boyfriend, but as her best friend. Now, her confidences were whispered into someone else's ear.

Jack's? Burk's?

As if his thoughts had conjured up the devil, Burk and Ken came striding into the coffeehouse.

They spotted Dawson and Jack and headed for their table.

Terrific, Dawson thought, his misery escalating. *Just when I thought this evening couldn't get any worse.*

"Hey, I'm glad to see you," Ken said eagerly, as he and Burk took the two empty seats at the table, where Dawson quickly introduced Ken and Burk to Jack.

"Did your bud Dawson here tell you how he saved our butt on a scene a few days ago?" Ken asked Jack.

"My bud here is notoriously modest," Jack replied.

"No kidding," Ken agreed. He held out a fist, and Dawson got that he was supposed to fist bump it.

So he did.

"I really have to thank you, man," Ken said. "Again."

"For what?" Dawson asked, puzzled.

"Well, you know how you said we could establish Lorell's personality quickly through something visual," Ken explained. "So, today, when we were doing a scene where Laken gets dripped to death, I had her kissing a photo of Burk here."

He hitched his thumb toward the gorgeous guy sitting next to him.

"And that accomplished—?" Dawson asked.

"Oh, I guess you never read the screenplay—using the term *screenplay* loosely—or you'd know," Ken said. "Laken's character is supposed to be the shy, quiet girl who is secretly in love with Tom, a.k.a. Burk."

"I see," Dawson said, his voice neutral.

"You should've heard Reginald going on and on about how brilliant Ken was to have thought of it," Burk said.

Ken looked guilty. "You know I wish I could give you the credit, Dawson."

"I understand," Dawson now assured him. Maybe he'd get good-guy points for helping Ken out without getting any of the glory, since he had a feeling he was heavily in the life-debit category for how he had treated Patrice that evening.

Jack looked at his watch. "They were supposed to start already," he noted impatiently.

Burk chuckled, as he reached for some popcorn. "Maybe Joey's back there freaking out. She told me she was so scared last time she could barely get her mouth to work."

"It's nice that Joey felt she could confide in you about that," Dawson said stiffly.

Burk nodded easily.

Clearly he had no idea what Dawson's relationship with Joey was.

"She's a great girl," Burk went on. "Special, ya know?"

"Actually, Dawson and I both know that," Jack said, bemused, as Burk picked up on none of their unspoken signals.

"I mean, how often do you meet a girl that great looking who is so totally natural?" Burk continued. "Unspoiled? All the girls I know in Hollywood think it's illegal not to begin a sentence with the word *I*."

"That's the opposite of Joey," Dawson declared.

Right after he said it, he decided he was insane, and that the last thing he needed to do was to confirm Burk's high opinion of Joey.

"I gotta tell you," Burk said, reaching for some more popcorn, "I'm really looking forward to tomorrow night."

Dawson and Jack's eyes met, as each suspected the unspoken part of that statement.

Just like in his interview with Arnie Bick, Dawson knew, instinctively, that he should keep his mouth shut.

Once again, he just couldn't do it.

"Why are you looking forward so much to tomorrow night?" he asked Burk, lightly.

Dawson could almost have said Burk's answer with him.

Burk smiled with anticipation. "Because I have a date with Joey."

Chapter 11

Dawson sat alone in a nearly empty Mondo Mocha, as some exhausted waitstaff finished cleaning up.

Once again, the Drips improv comedy group had been a huge success. And once again, Pacey was one of the major stars of the show. Objectively speaking, Joey had been the weakest performer up there. But she did manage to get a few laughs.

Not that Dawson had been able to enjoy the show. He would look from Joey up on stage, to Burk sitting across from him, and the contents of his stomach would gyrate like the cameras in *The Blair Witch Project*.

Now everyone had left—Joey had exited with Jack and not Burk—except for Pacey and Laken. The two of them were huddled in the far corner, deep in conversation.

A waitress wiped off Dawson's table, shooting him a pointed look that said, "Don't you have a life?"

Dawson checked his watch. It was really late. He'd promised Pacey he'd wait for him. But they both had to get up for another day of adolescent angst at Capeside High in the morning. And Pacey did not appear to be on the verge of wrapping things up with Laken.

Dawson was ready to pack it in.

He left a generous tip on the table and went over to Pacey and Laken. "Excuse me, but I'm gonna cut out, Pacey. Your show was great, by the way."

Laken stood up. "We're through," she told Dawson. "Hey, sorry I tied Pacey up for so long." She leaned down to kiss Pacey's cheek. "So, I'll see you on the set late tomorrow afternoon."

She grabbed her jacket, waved goodbye, and left.

"Now, that is one great girl," Pacey said, watching Laken leave. He gestured to the seat next to him. "Cop a squat, Dawson. It's time for your basic manly to manly talk."

"If the unspoken signals from the waitress over there are any clue," Dawson began, looking at the scowling waitress who was now wiping off his former table, "we should indulge in male bonding in another locale."

"The ever-observant, always-sensitive Dawson Leery speaks the truth." The two of them headed for the door.

Typical autumn New England weather had finally

set in, and they could see their breath in little puffs on the night air.

"So, I'm curious," Dawson said. "What was Laken talking to you about so earnestly?"

"It seems the lovely Laken is delusional enough to believe that I have actual talent," Pacey replied. He had neglected to bring a jacket to Mondo Mocha, so he rubbed his arms to warm them.

"That's no delusion, Pacey. You must know that. I mean, you were really incredible up there tonight."

"Do you have any idea what it's like?" Pacey asked. "What an incredible rush it is to make people laugh like that?" He swung around to walk backwards, so that he could gauge the reaction on Dawson's face.

"Not really," Dawson admitted.

"Well, it's . . . it's unbelievable," Pacey said. "Anyway, Laken was giving me all these tips on where to study improv. Needless to say, the closest sign of intelligent comedic life to Capeside is Boston."

"So, what are you going to do?" Dawson asked. They'd reached Pacey's dad's truck. Both got in.

"I'm sure the Chief of Police will declare me an emancipated minor, throw me a ten or twelve thou, and give me the unconditional love and support necessary for me to move to Boston and pursue my improvisational destiny," Pacey said sarcastically.

Dawson gave Pacey a quick glance as Pacey turned the ignition key.

"Seriously."

"Seriously. Per usual, I have absolutely no idea."

Even though it was cold out Pacey rolled down his window. "But enough about the soap opera of my life. Let's talk about yours. What did you think you were doing with the fair Patrice this evening?"

"Nothing," Dawson said evasively.

"Nothing? Let me get this straight. You blew her off?"

"I didn't exactly 'blow her off,' as you so inelo-quently put it," Dawson said defensively. "I don't think I was under any obligation to spend the evening with her."

"Let's review, shall we, Dawson?" Pacey asked in a singsong voice. "Joey blew *you* off. Then you blew *Joey* off. Then, out of the blue, whichever god watches over horny male teens everywhere sent you Patrice. She is fair, fulsome, and might I add, fine. And, most salient of all, *she wants you.* And you—"

"I already feel guilty enough, Pacey," Dawson in-terrupted, as Pacey made a right-hand turn. "It's not that I don't like her."

"So in what universe does it make sense for you to blow off a girl that you like?" Pacey asked in-credulously.

Dawson struggled to explain. "It's . . . bizarre. I mean sometimes, I really like her a lot. And other times, quite frankly, she makes my skin crawl."

"Dawson, Dawson, Dawson," Pacey chided him. "It's at moments like these that I long for the Pacey of old."

"I don't," Dawson said quickly.

Pacey ignored him. "Fortunately for you, Dawson, that Neanderthal lurks somewhere beneath the thin veneer of the new sensitive model. I'm feeling a *Three Faces of Eve* moment coming on."

Pacey's face changed completely, not unlike Joanne Woodward's face in the classic film when another one of Eve's multiple personalities took over.

"Dawson," Pacey groaned in deep voice, "it's me. Neanderthal Pacey. And I have only one question for you. Who cares if you're into the girl or not? *She* is into *you.* Meaning she will give you what Joey never gave you and what Eve tried to give you and you declined, a decision that I am sure you have regarded with frequent moments of regret. As the French say, it is better to have remorse than regret, so—"

"How do you know what the French say?" Dawson said, interrupting him.

"Andie told me that," Pacey admitted.

"Neanderthal Pacey needs to give up French culture and get back in his box," Dawson told him as they pulled up in front of Dawson's house.

"Neanderthal Pacey leaves you with these final words of wisdom: it feels great, it's guaranteed to make you go 'Joey *who?*' at least temporarily, and it clears up your skin. So, when you look at it like that, empty and meaningless sex can be kinda sacred."

Dawson rolled his eyes, as he got out of the truck.

"G'night, Pacey," Dawson called.

Pacey stuck his head out of the window. "I sincerely hope you remember the words of wisdom I've imparted to you tonight."

"Highly doubtful."

Neanderthal Pacey sighed dramatically. "There are none so blind as those who will not see. Plus, it's infinitely preferable to chokin' the ole—"

"Good *night*, Pacey." Dawson pushed Pacey's head back in the truck.

As he headed inside, Dawson found himself thinking about what Pacey had just told him. It made a certain amount of sense.

In some morally bankrupt way.

Yet Dawson knew that he could never bring himself to do it. Or to enjoy it. But even that knowledge didn't help him from feeling more alone than he had in a long, long time.

Jen and Joey stood in front of the mirror in Jen's bedroom, checking out their reflections. Joey had on an outfit that Jen had talked her into wearing for their double date—a strapless tube dress with strappy sandals.

Joey frowned at her image in the mirror and tugged at the top of her dress. She'd bought it on sale at the mall, the first new thing she'd bought in ages, compliments of the extra money she'd earned on the movie.

"Ken and Jen and Burk and Joey," Joey mused aloud. "It sounds like a bad movie from the sixties. Are you sure I don't scream of trying too hard?"

"You look hot," Jen told her. "And besides, you

already spent an afternoon rolling around in a sleeping bag with the guy."

Joey sat on Jen's bed. "That was Ashleigh in that sleeping bag, not Joey."

Jen gave her a sly smile. "So answer me this. Who got weak in the knees over it? Ashleigh, or Joey?"

"I suppose I did feel a certain . . . something," Joey admitted reluctantly. "But the fact that I'm still biologically linked to my hormones is just one of those little genetic quirks we all suffer through."

Jen laughed. "I wouldn't exactly call getting hot and bothered over Burk Flint 'suffering.' Especially when he was getting hot and bothered back over you. Do you know how many millions of girls would like to be in your tube dress right now?"

Joey folded her arms. "Am I supposed to care?"

"You are an endless source of amusement to me, Joey." Jen picked up a perfume bottle and sprayed her neck.

Jack stuck his head into the doorway. "Is this a girl-bonding thing in action, or can anyone join?"

"Come on in," Jen invited. "Tell Joey how great she looks."

Jack leaned against the door frame and nodded. "You do look great," he assured Joey, "though I should add the disclaimer that what I know about fashion would fit into a thimble."

Joey smiled at him. "It doesn't matter. You always did have great taste, Jack. So thank you."

"So, tonight's the big double date?"

Joey nodded. "I'm not sure it was such a good idea," she confessed.

"Honestly Joey, you and Dawson really do deserve each other," she groaned. "I never saw two people so willing to overanalyze the minutiae of their lives."

"Speaking of Dawson, I do share one of his concerns," Jack said.

Joey suddenly got very busy brushing her hair.

"Whatever it is, pretend you already shared it," Joey commented as her tone withered.

"Why not just get *I'm not really over him no matter how hard I pretend I am* tattooed onto your forehead, Joey?" Jen asked. "It'll fit in two rows of type."

"I really don't want to talk about it—"

"We're not talking about it," Jen pointed out. "But if you were really over him, it wouldn't bother you to hear what Jack has to say before you decide it's not genuine."

Joey sighed with irritation. "Fine. What is it?"

"It seems that while, from what little he knows of Burk, he's a decent-enough guy," Jack related. "However, he has also heard from various sources—one of those sources being Burk himself—that the guy is a player."

"I'm supposed to believe that Burk told Dawson that he's a player?" Joey asked dubiously.

Jack scratched his chin thoughtfully. And then he added, "Whatever else Dawson may be, I do believe that he is genuinely concerned about your well-being—"

"And I genuinely believe that at this point I wish he would do me the favor of keeping his genuine concern to himself," Joey replied.

"Then how about if it's *my* concern?" Jack asked.

"Noted." She said, as she looked back at the mirror and brushed her hair furiously.

But the harder she brushed, the more it felt like this thought was being brushed into her head: no matter where she went or what she did or who she did it with, one way or another, Dawson Leery always managed to be a part of it.

Dawson walked up to the front door of Patrice's house and knocked on the door.

Pacey was right. He'd really felt awful about having blown her off the night before. So when she'd come up to him at school that day to tell him she had a special surprise planned for him that same evening, he'd agreed on the spot to go out with her.

And, basically, he'd regretted it ever since.

Which probably makes me insane, stupid, or both, Dawson thought as he waited for Patrice to answer his knock.

A terrible possibility occurred to him.

What if I spend the rest of my life comparing everyone to Joey?

The front door of the Cape Cod–style home swung open, and there stood Patrice. She looked—well, there was really no other way to describe it—beautiful. Her glossy auburn hair was tied back with a ribbon, and she wore a lovely feminine dress that flowed to her knees.

"Come on in," she welcomed him, opening the outer screen door.

Dawson stepped into the foyer and looked around uncertainly. A family portrait of Patrice and her parents hung on one wall. Opposite it, in the same kind of frame, was a caricature of the same family portrait clearly penned by Patrice.

"You look beautiful," Dawson told her sincerely.

She glowed at the compliment. "And just to let you know what a special occasion this is. No sketch pad!" She held up her hands to show that they were empty.

A woman who looked like an older, heavier version of Patrice came into the foyer. "Well, I finally get to meet the infamous Dawson Leery. I've heard so much about you. I'm Patrice's mom, Estelle Reagen."

Dawson shook hands with her. "It's very nice to meet you, Mrs. Reagen."

She laughed. "I have to say, Patrice, he's a lot more polite than your last boyfriend." She turned to Dawson. "Please call me Estelle."

Boyfriend? Dawson thought with trepidation. It was another intestinal *Blair Witch* moment.

But Dawson had heard Estelle Reagen right.

Infamous.

Boyfriend.

I've heard so much about you.

Patrice and I are just friends was the disclaimer on the tip of his tongue. But he took one look at

Patrice's glowing face, and managed to keep his mouth shut.

"You ready?" Patrice asked Dawson.

He nodded. Not that he had any idea where it was that they were going.

Mrs. Reagen kissed her daughter's cheek. "Not too late, sweetie. It's a school night."

Patrice grabbed a sweater, then she and Dawson hurried out to his car.

"Where to, Madame?" Dawson asked, playfully. He was determined to have a good attitude and show Patrice a good time.

Instead of answering his question, Patrice merely gave him road directions. They ended up at a recently redeveloped strip mall near the beach. A uniformed valet stood in front of a new restaurant called Jezebel's.

Patrice told him to pull over.

He did.

"Here?" he asked. "I read about this place. Soul food and jazz, right? But it must cost a—"

Before Dawson could finish the statement, the valet had opened his car door and was waiting patiently for Dawson to exit the vehicle.

Dawson got out and put his car keys into the valet's extended palm. "Very good, sir," the valet told Dawson, handing him a claim ticket. Dawson stashed it self-consciously in his pants pocket before joining Patrice on the sidewalk.

He had thought perhaps that she was taking him out for a pizza. For burgers, maybe. But he had never, ever thought he'd be standing with her in front of what was probably the most expensive, exclusive restaurant in all of Capeside.

"Well, this is some surprise," Dawson told her uneasily, feeling monumentally uncomfortable . . . as well as monumentally guilty.

I would never take her to a place like this, he thought. *Never.*

She hooked an arm through his and led him through the front doors, which were held open by a uniformed doorman.

"And this is only the beginning of Dawson's evening of surprises," she said eagerly.

Inside, the restaurant was dark and expensive looking. A fire glowed warmly in a fireplace, and a jazz trio played unobtrusively as people dined in intimate leather booths.

"Do you have a reservation, sir?" the maître d' asked.

Patrice spoke up. "Yes, we do. Reagen. Party of two. *Patrice* Reagen."

"Ah, very good, Miss Reagen," the maître d' told her briskly. "The special table." He led Patrice and Dawson to a particular table in the middle of the room and then held chairs out for the two of them.

Of course, Dawson had to ask himself why the table was special. What could Patrice possibly have asked for? At this point, he wouldn't put anything past her. She could have ordered up belly dancers, a romantic violinist—almost anything.

Dawson looked around; then his eyes lit on

Patrice. He was just about to ask her when he realized he didn't have to say a word.

All he had to do was to look *past* her.

Which is exactly why he did.

And it was then that he realized he was looking at the back of the heads of Joey and Burk.

Chapter 12

"**W**hat are we doing here?" Dawson hissed at Patrice.

"We're having a really wonderful, special dinner, I hope," Patrice replied.

She reached for Dawson's hand. He snatched it away.

"Patrice, it has not failed to dawn on me that you brought me here precisely because Joey and Burk are here with Jen and Ken," Dawson said through clenched teeth. "And that you asked for a *special table*, meaning the table behind *their* table. Do you have any idea how embarrassing this is to me?"

"There's really no reason for you to be embarrassed, Dawson. And there's no reason for you not to be here with your girlfriend—"

"And *that's* another thing, you're *not my*—"

Dawson realized he was almost yelling, and lowered his voice immediately.

So far, it didn't seem as if the foursome at the table beyond theirs realized that he and Patrice were sitting right behind them. And he wanted that state of affairs to last for as long as humanly possible.

He did his best to look at her and not past her, to Joey laughing at something Burk had just said.

"Patrice, I like you." Dawson's voice was controlled.

Liar, he thought.

"We're friends," he continued.

Really big liar. I don't know what we are.

"We may or may not become more than that."

She gazed at him, her eyes two luminous pools of blue.

"But one thing I do know, Patrice," Dawson added softly, "is that these things don't happen overnight. And you can't force them to happen, either."

She nodded solemnly. "I'm willing to wait. Good things are worth waiting for."

Dawson had absolutely no idea how to respond to that line of reasoning.

What I really want to do is leave, Dawson thought. *This is the last place on earth that I want to be. And frankly, being in the last place on earth I want to be with Patrice makes the last place . . . more of a last place.*

So what would be worse? Tell her I want to leave or to stay under false pretenses?

Staying is definitely worse, he decided.

But before he could open his mouth to tell her, a tuxedoed waiter approached the table and handed them each oversized gilt-edged menus. Then the waiter reeled off, in a slightly Spanish accent, each of the specials, as if he were personally in love with every one of them.

Great, Dawson thought. *Now it's too awkward to leave.*

So he would have to do the next best thing.

He leaned close to Patrice. "I would really appreciate it if my friends did not know that we're here."

She cocked her head and regarded him curiously. "You're not ashamed to be seen with me, are you?"

"Patrice, you're beautiful, smart, talented—how could I possibly be ashamed to be seen with you?"

She seemed to think for a moment. "You know, you're right, Dawson. I rock. I'd go for me in a big way."

Dawson laughed in spite of himself. It never changed: every time he couldn't stand another moment of Patrice's company, she did or said something so wonderful that he found himself falling in like with her all over aga—

As Dawson watched, horrified, Patrice twisted around in her chair to tap Joey on the shoulder.

"Hi!"

I'm going to kill her, Dawson thought, wishing the opulent carpeted floor beneath him would open up so he could fall through rather than have to look at Joey now.

She was now staring at him, shocked.

So was Jen. As for Burk and Ken, they clearly didn't know what to think.

"You remember me, don't you?" Patrice asked them. "Patrice Reagen?"

Joey recovered slightly. "Oh, sure," she replied. Her eyes bore in on Dawson's.

"What a small world," she said sarcastically.

Dawson was prepared to be a gentleman rather than tell the truth—that he'd had absolutely nothing to do with he and Patrice being there.

But, once again, before he could open his mouth, Patrice began to speak.

"I totally have to tell you guys the truth," Patrice began. "See, I brought Dawson here to surprise him. He had no idea we were coming. And he also had no idea that you guys were gonna be here."

"Right," Joey nodded dubiously.

"Hey, what difference does it make?" Burk asked Joey. He looped his arm around her shoulders and smiled at Dawson. "The more the merrier, I say."

"Especially when it's the guy who saved our butts on *Dripping Red*," Ken added. "Do you guys want to come join us?"

"Yeah, there's plenty of room," Jen added quickly, a mischievous glint in her eye.

Dawson said no at the same time Patrice said yes.

But Patrice's voice was louder.

Much louder.

"You know, I really think it's a better idea if we—" Dawson began.

Too late. Patrice was already out of her chair and sliding in next to Ken and Jen.

Which left Dawson no choice but to slide in next to Joey and Burk.

And to prepare for what he was sure would be one uncomfortable evening.

He was right.

But Patrice appeared to be having the time of her life.

All through the dinner—raw oysters followed by salmon baked in a crust and sweet potato pie for dessert—she was the life of the party.

In fact, she had a tiny sketch pad stashed in her purse, which she took out in order to draw on-the-money caricatures of the various people in the restaurant, and then of all six of them. Herself included.

Everyone was having such a wonderful time that no one seemed to notice how quiet Dawson and Joey were.

When the jazz trio took the stage for the next set, Burk asked Patrice to dance.

Patrice looked over at Dawson. "Do you mind?"

"No, it's fine," Dawson managed.

It was much better than what he wanted to say.

Which was something like: "Why the hell would I mind?"

Or: "I wish the two of you would simply dance off into the sunset together. Forever."

Jen pulled Ken up to dance, leaving Dawson and Joey alone at the table.

"Having fun?" Joey asked sarcastically.

"Joey, this is, by far, one of the most uncomfortable experiences of my life," Dawson told her. "Surely you must know this wasn't my idea."

Joey scowled. "What I can't figure out, Dawson, is why your little friend seems so bent on throwing us together?"

"I can only guess that she thinks you're the reason I haven't exactly signed on as her soulmate."

"Am I?"

"You mean aside from the fact that she can be incredibly annoying? I don't know, Joey. I wish I knew what I wanted, but the truth is, I don't know that either. But I do know this much. I haven't stopped caring about you, anymore than you've stopped caring about me. And I also know that I want you to be happy."

"So do I," Joey said softly.

"So if being with Burk makes you happy . . ." Dawson got up and left the table.

Although it was a great rarity for Dawson to get in the last line with Joey, much less the last monologue, this time he was gone before she had a chance to offer a rejoinder.

When Patrice and Burk finished their dance, Patrice found Dawson standing near the front door of the restaurant.

"It's time for us to leave, Patrice," Dawson informed her.

"But wait, I didn't pay the check yet."

"I paid it," Dawson informed her, and then he led her outside into the brisk night air.

"Why did you do that?" Patrice protested. "It was supposed to be my surprise, my treat—"

"Plans changed," Dawson said tersely. He handed the claim check for his car to the valet, thinking that it was only by chance that he had so much money in his pocket. His mom had recently given him spending money for the entire month, and he had still had all of it.

Well, not anymore. Now, there was just a fistful of ones and some change.

Dawson was livid.

Not to mention broke.

But somehow, he thought, the whole thing would have been much worse if he had let her pay for it.

All the way back to Patrice's house, they didn't speak. Every time she tried to start a conversation, Dawson cut it off with a wall of silence.

He pulled his car into her driveway, parked, slammed on the parking brake, and went around to open the door for her. All he could think about was how quickly he wanted to be out of her company.

"Do you know how few guys do that anymore?" Patrice playfully asked him, as she got out of the car. "Too bad my mom didn't see you. She'd been so psyched that I finally have a boyfriend with manners."

"Patrice. I am *not your boyfriend!*" Dawson bellowed.

"Shhhh!" Patrice insisted. "Do you want to wake the whole neighborhood?"

"Sorry," Dawson said quickly.

She shrugged prettily. "Anyway, it's just a figure of

speech," she explained. "Boy, girl, out on a date, etcetera, etcetera."

He walked her to her front door without replying. He could hardly remember when he had last been so angry with someone who was not one of his parents.

"Want to come in?" she asked eagerly. "I have it on good authority that the parentals won't be home for at least another hour."

"No, I don't want to come in," Dawson snapped. "Patrice, what you did tonight was unbelievably manipulative. But you don't seem to realize that."

"Dawson, please, people manipulate people to get what they want all the time," Patrice said, not yet moving to open the front door.

"I don't. And I don't believe I could have respect for anyone who does."

"Really?" Patrice asked coolly. "You mean you never said or did anything to Joey to get her to say or do what you wanted her to say or do?"

Dawson knew he had.

Like the time he and Pacey had followed Joey and Jen to New York City.

Like the time he'd tried not to cast her in the lead of his short film, *Don and Dulcie*, even though she was by far the best person for the role, just because he didn't want to have to direct her in kissing scenes with some studly soap star.

Like the time . . .

Well.

There were just so many.

Guilt washed over him.

Patrice read it on his face and smiled triumphantly.

"So you see, Dawson, you kind of have to admire someone who wants someone else so much that she—or *he*—" she added pointedly, "is willing to do just about anything to get him—or her."

Dawson shook his head. "No. Actually, I don't. I'm not proud of the times I've been manipulative, Patrice. And besides, this isn't about me. It's about you."

She wrapped her arms around his neck. "Funny, I thought it was about me *and* you."

He extricated himself from her embrace. "The point is," Dawson said, "it's bad enough that I let you get away with what you got away with tonight. I'm not sure I understand why you did it. And I probably should have made a stand the moment I saw that Joey was at the next table, too, but—"

"I'm the kind of girl that likes to be direct about things," Patrice explained. "I thought it would do Joey a world of good to see you with me again. And you a world of good to see Joey with Burk. All I was doing was being up front. Totally."

She moved closer to him· again, smiling seductively.

"Besides, I know you like me more than you let on, Dawson. After all, you're the one who told me how wonderful I am."

As Dawson gazed down at her, the weirdest thing happened.

Her face morphed into Glenn Close's from *Fatal Attraction*.

He quickly stepped away from her, half-expecting her to scream, "I will not be ignored!" And then he started backing down the front walkway.

"I suggest we do a lot of thinking about this, Patrice," Dawson called to her, now halfway down the walk. "Private thinking. As in we don't speak to each other for a while."

"I totally understand, Dawson," Patrice called back to him. "And I apologize if I did or said anything tonight that offended you."

Dawson made it all the way to his car, and had the driver's side door open, before she spoke again.

"Dawson? One last thing. I had the greatest time tonight. And I want you to know . . ."

Dawson waited. It was coming.

And here it was.

"That I'll be dreaming about you."

Chapter 13

Dawson lay on his bed, his eyes fixed on the ceiling, thinking about how it had become a familiar sight to him of late.

It had been a week and a half since his nightmarish date with Patrice. Eleven days, actually. And still, flashes of the movie of it ran over and over in the theater of his mind.

That moment, when he'd realized he was looking at the back of Joey's head at the restaurant.

That moment, when Joey and her friends had all turned around and realized Dawson was at the table behind them. With Patrice.

That moment, when he knew they thought that coming to the restaurant had been his idea.

The day after that fiasco, he'd had a chance to explain the whole thing to Jen. Jen had promised to explain it all to Joey. And—allegedly anyway—she had.

Whether or not Joey believed him, however, was a whole different story.

Dawson closed his eyes, and tried to figure out when his world had turned into Dawson-Leery-on-the-outside-looking-in.

On second thought, yes, he could. It was one single moment.

It was the moment he'd looked at the posted lists of jobs for the movie.

It was that same day Patrice Reagen had come into his life.

Dawson sighed, and thought about how he'd spent the last eleven days avoiding her. Sure, he saw her at school—they had a couple of classes together, so there was really no getting around it—but other than that, he ran from Patrice like the proverbial plague.

The first few days, she had left more than a dozen messages on his answering machine, none of which he returned. Since then, the messages were fewer and farther between.

He was looking forward to the day when they ended completely.

He only hoped he'd live long enough to see it.

There was a knock on his door frame. Dawson turned his head to see Pacey. His friend carried a paper sack in one hand and a video in the other.

"Beware of geeks bearing gifts," Pacey quipped. "Or, even better: I come to bury Dawson, definitely not to praise him."

He threw the paper bag at Dawson's abs.

"Did I know you were coming over?" Dawson asked.

"Consider it a mission of mercy. You, my friend, are pathetic. And, as a member of the International Society of the Formerly Pathetic, I am all too familiar with this state of being."

Pacey plopped down on the end of the bed as Dawson sat up and peered inside the paper bag.

"Junk food?" Dawson asked. "Your mercy mission is bringing me *junk food?*"

"Not junk food, Dawson. Doritos. There's a difference. Not to mention a video," Pacey added, thrusting a blue box at Dawson.

Dawson held it sideways and read the title. "*Fatal Attraction*? Highly amusing, Pacey." He handed Pacey back the video.

"Hey, where's your sense of humor?" Pacey asked. "After hearing your blow-by-blow description of your scintillating new homage to the late, great Louis Malle, *My Dinner with Patrice*, I decided what you need to do is to laugh about it."

"Ha-ha. Satisfied?"

Dawson fired the bag of junk food on his dresser, where it landed with a crack.

"When I was little," Pacey observed, "I left you the broken potato chips. Yet we were best friends. And now, as your once and future best friend, it is my duty to inform you that you need to get a life in a major way."

"Should I be taking notes?"

"It's eight o'clock at night, Dawson," Pacey continued, ignoring Dawson's sarcasm. "But where do I find you? Big shock. In your room. Solo. Which is where, sadly, I always find you. The only variation on this theme appears to be whether you are (a) watching a video, (b) working on the first page of a new screenplay, or (c) reliving—yet again—your restaurant meal of a lifetime."

"All artists spend time alone, Pacey," Dawson said defensively. "Besides, all of the people closest to me have been busy working on a film in which I am not involved."

Pacey held up one finger. "Correction. You are involved, albeit secretly. Remember, you gave Ken advice three different times on ways to improve what is still an execrable little B movie, made slightly less execrable by your uncredited assistance."

"Well, in that case, I won't shed any tears that I can't put it on my resume," Dawson said.

Pacey got the bag of junk food and yanked out the bag of Doritos. He shoved a handful into his mouth. "The ever-lovely Patrice asked me about you at school today."

Dawson groaned. "She hasn't called me in twenty-four whole hours. I consider that a hopeful sign that she has moved on."

"Doubtful. In fact, she's added a character based on you to her cartoon strip. And might I say you don't come off well."

Pacey held the Doritos out to Dawson.

Dawson shook his head. "Maybe she'll work all of her hostility toward me out in her art," he said hopefully. "That would be progress."

"Well, I have a feeling you're just avoiding the inevitable," Pacey said, through another mouthful of chips. "What you should do is just pick up the phone, call the psycho—I mean girl—and tell her that you're very sorry but whatever it is that she thinks existed between the two of you no longer exists."

"Weren't you the guy counseling me to go for the gusto with her?" Dawson reminded him. "If I had followed your advice, she'd probably have me handcuffed to a bed somewhere right now."

"Now, *that* you might enjoy," Pacey said. "Anyway, enough about Patrice. There's only one more day of shooting on the picture. After that, everything around here should get back to normal."

"Whatever that is," Dawson muttered. He had no idea what "normal" was anymore.

It wasn't Dawson and Joey, that was for sure. It wasn't the wonderful Leery family, that was equally for sure. It wasn't even Dawson and Pacey. It seemed like Pacey was spending more time consoling Joey.

"What will make my life normal again?" Dawson asked himself.

Pacey raised an arched eyebrow. "Going for one of those internal voiceover monologue pity party things, Dawson, that filmmakers use when they're not good enough to tell their story with pictures?"

Dawson made a decision.

Pacey was right. He really was pathetic. Sitting home feeling sorry for himself. Not going out for fear he'd run into Patrice.

Well, all that was about to change.

Dawson got up, shoved his wallet into the back pocket of his pants, and turned back to Pacey. "Well?"

"Well what?"

"Well, let's get the hell out of here," Dawson told him.

"Now you're talking." Pacey grabbed the Doritos and the two of them headed downstairs. "The night is young and so are we. Not to mention the chief of police is occupied in a county far, far away this evening, minus his beloved truck. Which is parked in front of your house even as we speak. I say we make the most of it."

"Beach volleyball?" Dawson asked, as Pacey drove, heading toward the beach.

"*Night* beach volleyball," Pacey explained. "Most of the people involved in the movie are playing. I heard they were making a bonfire, too, and they painted the volleyball with some kinda day-glo stuff so it would glow in the dark."

"So when were you gonna tell me about this?"

"Well, if I couldn't get you out of your funk and/or your room," Pacey said, "I wasn't going to tell you at all. Hence the junk food and video. Backup."

Dawson was touched. "You mean you were going to miss the festivities here so you could hang out with me in my alleged hour of need?"

"Sometimes the wonderfulness that is me overwhelms," Pacey joked, stopping for a red light.

"And before you add your next Dawson-like comment, which will be something about how you don't want to horn in on a group of which you are not a part, let me just say: bull. Leave it at that, shall we?"

"Consider it left," Dawson said, thinking that at least the odds were good that Patrice wouldn't be at the beach.

Whatever, Dawson thought, staring out the window. *I can't spend my life avoiding every situation that makes me uncomfortable.*

Pacey turned onto the street that bordered the beach.

Time for a thought change, Dawson decided. *Preferably about someone not me. And not remotely involved with me.*

"You given any more thought to Pacey Witter, new King of Improvisational Comedy?" Dawson asked, as Pacey found a place to park.

"It's still hard for me to believe that I'm actually good at it," Pacey admitted. He backed into a spot. "But then, it's still hard for me to believe that I'm actually good at anything."

"You were really funny doing improv," Dawson insisted, as they both got out of the truck and walked toward the beach. "In my unbiased opinion, you have a lot of talent."

"I guess all those years as class clown paid off," Pacey said ironically.

"So, you thinking about taking that class in Boston that Laken told you about?"

Pacey shrugged. "I don't know, man. It's hard for

me to think about making any real decisions now until I get back on an even keel."

Dawson's eyes slid over to him. "Well, let me just tell you what I know you'd be telling me. You can't let decisions about your life be hampered by ex-girlfriends."

"You know, I hate it when you throw my sensitive and brilliant words of wisdom back in my face," Pacey said.

They heard the music blaring a thousand feet away before they reached the party. Hip-hop blared from a portable sound system. And a couple dozen people were playing volleyball by the light of a puny-looking bonfire.

"Now that is one weenie bonfire," Pacey observed. "Hey!" he yelled to the volleyball players. "Didn't any of you get a merit badge in camping? I'm ashamed to call you Boy Scouts!"

"Shut up and get in the game," Laken commanded, as someone spiked the ball over the net. "You too, Dawson."

Pacey joined one team, Dawson the other. To his relief, neither Joey nor Patrice were anywhere in sight.

Of course, he couldn't help noticing that Burk was nowhere in sight, either.

After a while, Dawson got into the game, which gave his mind a much needed rest. It was, quite frankly, a relief. So, even after his side lost the volleyball game, assisted in defeat by his decidedly minimal volleyball skills, Dawson actually felt much better.

He dropped to the sand near Jen, Ken, and a few others who'd been playing.

"Glad you came out, Dawson," Jen told him. "I've kinda been missing you lately."

"I've kinda been missing you, too," Dawson replied. "I've been missing a lot of people. And things."

"I can't say I'll be upset when we wrap this movie tomorrow," Ken admitted. "Except for not getting a chance to spend even more time with certain people, that is." He looked fondly over at Jen.

Jen smiled at him. "Right back atcha, big guy."

Ken turned to Dawson. "Hey, can I talk to you a minute?"

"Sure."

Ken got up, so Dawson did, too. Evidently whatever Ken wanted to talk to him about he wanted to say privately. Dawson joined Ken and they strolled slowly down the beach, away from the crowd.

"So listen, Dawson," Ken began, when they were out of anyone's earshot. "I want to thank you again for the ideas you gave me on the movie. Basically, we used all of 'em. I'm only sorry that there's no credit where credit is due. Not in money or even in your name on the screen."

"I suppose all I can say is that I appreciate your appreciation," Dawson said.

Ken shoved his hands into his pockets. "I've been thinking for a while now about what I could do to repay you. So, any ideas?"

"There's really no need for—"

"Hey, it's rare in this business for someone to help

someone else out," Ken insisted. "Especially without getting anything in return. Everyone knows you got screwed out of working on this film. If you don't mind, I think I figured out a way to make it up to you."

Dawson waited, curious.

"Mike Bick, the executive producer of the film, is flying on the red-eye to Boston, so he can see the rough cut of the film," Ken went on. "I couldn't tell him the truth about your contributions—frankly, his sniveling little cousin Arnie is taking full credit for your ideas. And I suppose that blood is thicker than water."

"Especially if it's *Dripping Red* blood," Dawson put in.

Ken chuckled. "Yeah. Anyway, Mike is a good guy. I've worked with him on three films now, and he trusts me. I've already told him I met a kid here who is incredibly talented. So I think he wants to meet you."

Dawson was so surprised, he stopped walking.

Ken did, too.

"Wait. You're telling me he wants to meet me because I have talent?" Dawson asked. "You did that for me?"

"It's the least I could do," Ken said. "Besides, I was telling the guy the truth."

Dawson was overwhelmed. "I hardly know what to say. Except that it was incredibly nice of you."

Ken grinned again. "Well, I should be completely honest with you. It was your friend Jen's idea. She rules. When she turns eighteen, make sure she calls me."

"Knowing Jen, you'll be on a waiting list." Dawson held his hand out, and shook Ken's hand. "Listen, no matter whose idea it was, you still had to agree to it, and you had to implement it. So, thank you."

"You're welcome."

"As far as Jen goes," Dawson said, "you're right about her. She does rule. In fact, I think I'll go tell her so myself."

Chapter 14

Dawson and Jen strode into the lobby of the Capeside Inn. He checked his watch—it was 11:50 A.M. His appointment with executive producer Mike Bick was at noon. He'd gotten the call that morning from Bick's assistant, asking Dawson to come meet with Mike at his hotel.

Dawson hadn't complained about the lack of prep time, or about anything else for that matter. He was thrilled to get the phone call. And, fortunately for him, it was Saturday, so he didn't have to deal with the messy problem of cutting school.

As soon as he'd hung up with Mike's assistant, he'd called Jen. She didn't have to be at the set until the afternoon, when they'd be packing everything up and shutting everything down. So she'd immediately volunteered to come over and help Dawson get ready for his big meeting.

And then she'd insisted on coming with him, for moral support.

"Are you sure I shouldn't have worn a sports jacket and a tie?" Dawson asked Jen, for the third time. He wore the chinos and denim shirt she'd suggested he wear. He'd actually tucked his shirt in—which felt very weird—instead of leaving it open over a T-shirt.

"Trust me, Dawson," Jen said. "No one in L.A. wears a tie except to their own funeral. Maybe. You're fine."

"Well, he told me to come right up. He's in the penthouse," Dawson said nervously. "But then, I suppose the penthouse is a given in his income bracket. Come to think of it, I imagine the so-called penthouse at the Capeside Inn is a major comedown in his lifestyle."

"Dawson?"

"Yes?"

Jen patted his arm. "You're babbling."

"Right." Dawson hugged Jen, then walked to the elevator.

Funny, Dawson thought as the elevator headed up, *I've lived in Capeside my entire life, and I've never been to the penthouse here. I vaguely recall my father saying he and his friends rented it the night of their senior prom. Weird to think that next year it will be my senior prom. Weirder to think about what happens after that.*

He got off at the top floor and knocked on the only door in sight.

It opened.

There stood Patrice.

Dawson's jaw fell open. This couldn't be happening.

"The particular shade of green on your face clashes with the blue of that denim," Patrice observed. "As an artist, I'm very sensitive to color. Come in."

Dumbfounded, Dawson stepped into what looked like a large living room. Past that was a hallway, at the end of which was a closed door. No one else was visible.

"What are you doing here?" he hissed.

"I'm Mike Bick."

Dawson's jaw fell open.

"I wish you could see yourself," Patrice said, laughing. "God, I slay me. You can start breathing again, Dawson. I'm only joking. I stopped by to do you a favor."

Dazed, Dawson sat on the taupe leather couch. "I know I'm going to regret asking, Patrice, but what's the favor?"

She sat next to him. "Well, it's like this. Mike has an assistant. Claudia. Claudia's sister lives in Capeside. In fact, she's the banquet manager here."

"I'm assuming this is all eventually going to make sense?" Dawson asked warily.

"Hang in there. Anyway, Claudia's sister is a friend of my parents. And Claudia and her sister were over last night. Claudia mentioned that she was supposed to call some kid this morning who was supposed to be this film genius to set up an appointment for this kid to see Mike.

"Well, I didn't have to be a rocket scientist to know who she was talking about, Dawson," Patrice concluded.

"But that doesn't explain why you're here," Dawson said.

Patrice crossed her legs and sat back on the couch. "It's not so complicated, really. When Claudia mentioned she was setting up your appointment for noon, I got an idea. I came over at eleven-thirty and had a little chat with Claudia. I explained that you were my boyfriend, and then I went on and on about how incredibly talented you are, and then I asked if I could go in and tell Mike the same thing."

Dawson smacked himself in the forehead. "Please tell me this is a joke."

"No, no," Patrice assured him. "There's really no need to thank me. You really are a film genius. And anything I could do to be of help—"

"*Help?*" Dawson echoed incredulously. "You call that *help?*"

Patrice sighed. "I know, you're disappointed because you already figured out that I didn't get in to see Mike. He's been watching rough cuts all morning. In fact, he isn't back yet."

Dawson closed his eyes. "Thank God."

When he opened his eyes again, Patrice's face was only inches from his. "I know you'd do the same thing to help out my cartooning career, Dawson," she murmured. "And I want you to know, I understand why you've been avoiding me."

He slid away from her. "You do?"

She nodded, staring deeply into his eyes. "When feelings come on so hard and strong, they can be overwhelming."

At that moment, Dawson did have overwhelming feelings. But not the kind Patrice was talking about.

He squelched them.

I have to figure out how to get her out of this room, he thought, *before—*

Before Dawson could finish his thought, the door down the hall opened, and an attractive middle-aged woman entered.

"Oh, Patrice!" the woman exclaimed, smiling. "This must be your boyfriend, Dawson. I've heard so much about you." She held her hand out to Dawson. "I'm Claudia Pearson, Mr. Bick's assistant."

Dawson stood up to shake hands. "It's nice to meet you. And thank you so much for setting up this appointment for me."

"My pleasure. Especially since your Patrice's boyfriend. Patrice's parents have done so much for my sister since she moved to Capeside. So I'm really pleased for the opportunity to return the favor."

Dawson nodded, numbly. He knew he was being a total hypocrite. But he wasn't about to correct Claudia's impression that he was Patrice's boyfriend. He had certainly suffered for that incorrect title. So, he rationalized that profiting from it just a little would just kind of even everything out.

"Mr. Bick called about fifteen minutes ago," Claudia explained. "He said things were winding up and he was on his way. Can I get you anything while you're waiting?"

"No, thank you," Dawson said. Patrice took his hand. Dawson tried to smile.

"Young love," Claudia sighed. "I remember what that's like. Well, I have a few things to do, so I'll just leave you two lovebirds alone until Mr. Bick shows up."

She went back down the hall.

As soon as she left, Dawson dropped Patrice's hand.

"Don't you think it would be a good idea for you to leave?" he suggested. "I mean, it's not very professional to bring a . . . friend . . . along on an interview."

"Oh no," Patrice said breezily, as she plopped back down on the couch, patting the space next to her. "Want to get up close and personal?"

"This is not the time or the—"

The front door opened. A good-looking guy of medium height stepped inside. He was no older than twenty-five.

"Mr. Bick?" Dawson asked, standing up quickly, as did Patrice.

"Please, call me Mike," the producer said. "When you say 'Mr. Bick,' I look for my dad."

"I might be a little confused," Dawson admitted. "Are you the executive producer, or would that be your father?"

Mike laughed. "My dad's in the shoe business. But credit where credit is due: he loaned me the money to start Bick Productions. At zero interest, I might add."

"Well, there's no business like shoe business!" Patrice quipped. She quickly introduced herself, explaining her relationship to both Claudia and Dawson.

"Claudia's the best assistant I've ever had," Mike said, "so any friend of hers is a friend of mine. You know, I've heard a lot about you, Dawson. Ken went on and on about how talented you are. He's got a great eye. And this is the first time he's ever been this enthusiastic about someone who isn't knee-deep in professional credits."

"That was really nice of him," Dawson replied. "I only hope I can live up to the advance billing."

Mike nodded. "I've got a good feeling about you. So, would you like to come back to what passes as my office, and we can talk a bit."

"That would be great," Dawson replied.

"Be nice to him," Patrice warned Mike. "Dawson's going to be the next Spielberg-Truffaut-Welles all in one. Which means someday, if you're lucky, you'll be working for him."

Dawson winced.

If I kill her now, no jury of my peers will convict me, he thought.

Before Mike could respond, the door opened again. In walked Arnie Bick.

My life is now officially over, Dawson thought. *I'm changing my identity. In my new life, I'll be Dawson Bronson. Starring in my very own version of* Death Wish 7.

"You?" Arnie exclaimed, as soon as he saw Dawson. "What the hell are you doing here?"

Claudia came down the hall, hesitating when she heard Arnie's raised voice.

"Make me some coffee, doll," Arnie told her, speaking to Claudia, but not taking his eyes off Dawson. "And don't skimp on the Kreamerino. I'm waiting for an answer."

Dawson mentally scrambled for some way, any way, to salvage this situation.

Nothing came to mind.

"I have an appointment with Mike," Dawson finally said.

Mike looked confused. "Is there some problem, Arnie?"

"What the hell are you seeing this little twerp for?" Arnie asked his cousin.

"You can't call him a twerp," Patrice insisted.

"Let's leave the name calling out of it," Mike suggested. "Ken says Dawson has more potential in the business than anyone he's met in ages."

Arnie laughed derisively, his outsized Adam's apple bobbing up and down. "It's a good thing I'm here to set you straight, then," he said. "This kid is all hat, no cattle, if you catch my drift. He was so obnoxious and full of himself when I interviewed him that I didn't even think about hiring him. Even as an unpaid gofer!"

Dawson couldn't take it anymore. Besides, he figured he had nothing to lose.

"With all due respect," Dawson began, "I am decidedly not, as you so cleverly put it, all hat, no cattle. I know a great deal about film. And while I've no doubt that I have a great deal more to learn, I would theorize that the reason you didn't hire me for the movie is because it was so patently obvious that I know more about film than you do."

Patrice actually applauded.

She might as well have been nailing his coffin shut.

Mike wearily rubbed one hand over his face. "This is getting a bit complicated. Arnie is my cousin and my business partner. And, while we don't always see eye to eye, he's been hands-on for this picture, not me. So it's kinda tough for me to supercede his authority."

Claudia silently handed Arnie a cup of coffee and hurried away again.

Mike turned to a smug Arnie. "Are you sure about this? Ken has a killer taste, you know."

Arnie sipped his steaming coffee. "Hey, who you gonna believe? Your semitalented A.D. or me?"

"I can see this is an extremely awkward situation," Dawson said. "All I can do now is to say thank you for trying to help me, Mr. Bick. Obviously, I inadvertently made an enemy of your cousin. I suppose there's a lesson in that for me."

He held his hand out to Mike and they shook. "Thanks again," Dawson said. "Best of luck with Bick Productions."

Dawson headed for the door, and Patrice followed him.

"You're going to be sorry," she told the Bicks, over her shoulder.

When Dawson opened the door, Ken and Jen were on the other side.

"This is getting rather Marx Brothers–esque," Dawson said. "So my next line must be: 'what are you doing here?'"

Jen and Ken didn't answer. Instead they stepped into the room. Mike and Arnie hurried over to them.

"Here's the short explanation of a complex story," Ken told Mike, not letting Arnie get in the first word. "Jen saw Arnie on his way up here. She called my room, and we decided to stop in and add our two cents to the mix."

"Oh, I see, now. Well, if that's to clear things up," Mike said, "it doesn't. And frankly, I'm much too busy for all this drama."

"Mr. Bick, I'm Jen Lindley, Ken's assistant. I used to be Arnie's assistant. I'll make it short and sweet. Arnie took credit for Dawson's ideas on the movie. It's as simple as that."

Mike looked at Ken, a question in his eyes.

"At the risk of digging my own professional grave," Ken said, "She's right."

"You don't really expect my cousin to believe these teenagers over me, do you?" Arnie sputtered.

"Look, this isn't the Bible, and I'm not Solomon," Mike said. "I'm putting this on hold indefinitely. I have a movie to wrap and a company to run. Arnie, get your butt into my office."

With that, Mike turned and walked away.

The last Dawson, Patrice, Jen, or Ken saw of the Arnster, he was hurrying after Mike, his Kreamerino-laced coffee sloshing onto the floor.

Chapter 15

The time since he'd first heard about *Dripping Red*, Dawson decided, had been—not counting his various break-ups with Joey—the worst days of his life.

But today had to be the worst of the worst.

All of his friends were at the Inn, at the wrap party.

His opportunity to have Mike Bick become his mentor had been ruined by Arnie.

And Patrice was back.

In fact, at that moment, Dawson and Patrice were strolling along the beach, down by the water. After leaving Mike's office, Dawson had gone home to lick his wounds. Hours later, he'd called Patrice and asked if they could meet and talk.

She'd been only too eager to agree.

As much as she made him crazy, Dawson didn't want to hurt her feelings any more than he had to. What had she done that was so awful, really, besides liking him too much and too soon?

"I was thinking we could hit this obscure museum in Boston next weekend," Patrice told him as they strolled along. "They're doing a retrospective of R. Crumb cartoons. And after that we could go out for seafood. I know this killer little restaurant. It looks like a dump, but—"

"Patrice." Dawson stopped walking and turned to her. "We need to talk."

He walked over to a railroad tie that had drifted up on the beach and sat down. She sat, too.

"That sounded ominous," she laughed nervously.

Dawson shook his head. "Not ominous, but . . . look, Patrice, you are an incredible girl. But I'm not ready for a relationship."

"Dawson, you only think you're not ready—"

"What I think is that I know what I want better than you know what I want," Dawson said firmly. "Believe me, I recognize all the superior things about you. I'm beyond flattered that you seem to like me as much as you do. But you deserve to be with someone who can return your enthusiasm. Right now, Patrice, I just can't."

She reached for his hand. "All right. I'll wait then. You'll get Joey Potter out of your system. You'll see."

"Sadly, or maybe maddeningly, I will never get Joey out of my system. She's a part of me, and she always will be, whether we're together or not."

Patrice arched an eyebrow. "Makes it kind of tough on the future bride, doesn't it?"

"I get freaked out thinking about next week, next month, next year," Dawson told her. "Beyond that is too complex and confusing for me to even begin to contemplate."

Dawson stood up. He had nothing more to say.

"Well, I guess you just shot me down, Dawson," Patrice said, rising, too. "I can't say it doesn't hurt."

Tears came to her eyes.

Dawson felt terrible. He had to resist the urge to apologize for hurting her, to reach for her, comfort her, and tell her it was all just a big misunderstanding.

But the truth was, he knew he'd be doing that more for himself than for her. So that he could still be the white knight on the horse, saving the damsel in distress.

She fisted the tears off her face. "If you don't mind, I think I'll walk by myself for awhile. I can get home fine. It's not far."

"Are you sure that's what you want to do?"

She nodded. "Who knows? I hear pain fuels one's art. Maybe I'll get some incredibly vicious and hilariously funny cartoons out of this." She slowly backed away from him.

"See ya around, Dawson."

"See ya."

She turned, and he watched her walk away.

That was exactly what he wanted, wasn't it? Then why did it still make him feel like crap?

He stood there for a long time, deep in thought, until a loud honking from behind startled him.

He turned. There was Pacey, leaning on the horn of his father's truck. He pulled up alongside Dawson. Inside was not only Pacey, but Jen. Ken, Laken, Burk, and three other extras Dawson didn't know by name were in the flatbed.

Pacey rolled down the window and leaned over Jen. "We stopped by your house," he told Dawson. "Your dad told us where to find you. Your chariot awaits, sir."

"What are you guys doing?" Dawson asked, confused but happy to see his friends. "Aren't you supposed to be at the wrap party?"

"Frankly, we decided we would prefer a small wrap party," Jen told him. "Invitation only. You just got yours."

Jen opened the door and pulled Dawson in.

It turned out the small and private wrap party was at Mondo Mocha. Inside, a couple of dozen people from the film were in party mode, dancing to hip-hop cranked to eleven.

With great relief, Dawson saw that Arnie wasn't there.

"Come on, Dawson," Jen said, grabbing his hand. "Dance with me."

The music changed to something slow and sultry, and Dawson took Jen in his arms.

"I really want to thank you again for everything you did for me," Dawson told Jen, as they swayed. "It went above and beyond the call of friendship."

"Oh, I'm sure I'll more than make up for it by doing something really stupid and tacky in the future," Jen replied lightly. "Ugly little scene in Mike's suite today, by the by, huh?"

"I've already put it behind me," Dawson assured her.

Jen grinned. "Liar. I know you like a book I've read too many times, Dawson."

"That's not exactly complimentary."

"Well, then, let me add a favorite, well-loved book." She rested her head against his shoulder. "I couldn't help notice you seemed to have lost an appendage named Patrice."

"We seem to have severed our nonrelationship."

"Because of your nonrelationship with Joey?"

"Very funny. No, I have a feeling Patrice isn't the right girl for me under any circumstances."

Ken came over and stole Jen away, and Dawson wandered upstairs to the small, and as yet unused, balcony. It was filled with rows of old theater seats.

He sat there in the back, contemplating the nature of *The Life of Dawson*, when he heard voices a few rows in front of him. It was so dark in the balcony, that obviously whoever was talking didn't know he was there.

"It's not that I don't like you, Burk."

Dawson knew that voice anywhere. Everywhere. Joey.

"What, then?" Burk asked. "I thought we were having a kick-butt time together."

"We did," Joey replied. "I mean, we do, but—"

Dawson waited, breathless. He knew the right thing to do was leave. But if he got up, they'd hear him. Which meant Joey would think he was spying on her.

Again.

"The best way I can explain it—which probably isn't very good, but it's the best I can do—is to say that I'm not ready for a relationship with anyone right now," Joey struggled to explain.

"Relationship?" Burk echoed. "Pretty heavy-duty word, there. I thought we were just hanging out."

"Oh really? So, do you always try to get girls into bed when you're 'just hanging out'?"

Dawson had to stifle both impulses: to laugh, and to punch out Burk.

"I'm not exactly hard up, Joey," Burk said, more amused than angry. "I think you're terrific. I thought you were as into me as I'm into you, but if not, no hard feelings."

"Meaning don't leave angry, just leave?" Joey asked.

"Meaning I'm not some high school kid trying to hide his anatomical reaction to *Playboy*. I just keep forgetting how young you are."

Joey got up. "Trust me, Burk. I'm much older than you think. There's someone in my life—I'm not with him right now—but he's still and always will be in my life. And that relationship, whatever it is, has an unwritten final chapter. Which kind of emotionally supersedes my giving it up to a hot guy who's here today and gone tomorrow. Even if the hot guy is you."

Burk got up too, and held out his arms. Joey stepped into them.

Dawson's hands white-knuckled around the armrests of his seat.

"You're something else, Joey Potter," Burk said

softly. "I have to tell you, it's not every day I get shot down."

"So happy to be a refreshing little change in your life," Joey replied.

They hugged, and Dawson mentally begged Joey not to kiss him.

So many of the things Dawson had wished for lately hadn't happened, but finally he had a wish come true.

Hours later, Dawson sat with Pacey and Jen amid the party ruins. Jen's shoes were off and her feet up on the table. A few other diehards were still dancing.

"Killer party," Pacey observed.

Dawson was quiet, staring off into the distance.

"Penny for your thoughts, Dawson," Jen said.

"Well, here's what I was thinking today," Dawson began slowly. "Over the past few weeks, all of the people closest to me—not counting my parents, of course—have been involved in an all-consuming project with which, for all practical purposes, I was not involved. And it started me thinking. One year of high school after this year. Then we all go off to different colleges. And it seemed to me it would feel not unlike what I've felt over the past few weeks. Only it would feel that way forever."

Total silence, as Pacey and Jen took this in.

"Well, I gotta tell you, Dawson," Pacey finally said, "you sure know how to kill a party."

"It's just that everything changes," Dawson said. "And there's nothing we can do about it."

"You're not exactly a fatalist, Dawson," Jen observed. "We don't necessarily all have to drift apart. We definitely have a choice in the matter."

Dawson cocked his head at her. "Who you trying to convince, Jen? Me? Or you?"

"Geez, someone stick Ani DiFranco in the sound system," Pacey groaned. "We need a soundtrack for this level of angst."

"Pacey?"

It was Joey, standing behind them.

"Do you think you could give me a ride home? I kinda let Burk go without me."

"No prob," Pacey replied. "Although I feel morally obligated to point out that Mr. Leery will be riding in the same vehicle."

"I think I can deal with that," she said softly. Her eyes met Dawson's. "After all, he already sat in on my big breakup with Burk."

Talk about shock.

Joey had known he was up in the balcony all along.

And then came shock number two.

She smiled at him and walked away.

Well.

Somehow the night didn't look quite as dark after all, Dawson decided.

Ken came over and touched Jen's shoulders. "They're ready to close this place down."

Jen nodded and looked up at him. "Don't you think it's time to give Dawson his big surprise?"

Ken pulled something out of his back pocket.

A white envelope. He handed it to Dawson.

"Does it come with an explanation?" Dawson asked.

"This afternoon, I got to thinking," Ken began. "It was making me nuts that Arnie was getting away with his scam—taking credit for your ideas. So I decided to go back to Mike and talk with him. But this time when I went to talk with him, I had a backup. A letter attesting to your invaluable artistic input signed by a whole lot of people."

Dawson was flabbergasted. He opened the envelope. Inside was a copy of that letter.

And another one.

On Bick Productions stationery, it was a handwritten note from Mike Bick, inviting Dawson to call him in New York.

"I can't believe you did this."

"A lot of people wanted to set things right," Ken explained. "Me too."

"I want you to know, Dawson," Pacey said, "I signed not only as myself, but also under three or four cleverly created pseudonyms, with the theory that there's power in numbers."

Jen leaned over to Dawson and kissed his cheek. "Congrats, Dawson. You just got the big Hollywood contact you so richly deserve."

"Thank you just seems so inadequate," Dawson said. "But . . . thank you. Really."

Jen jumped up. "What say we cut Dawson off now before he launches into one of his psychobabble moments," she suggested. "I'm gonna grab my stuff. Meet you all at the front door."

As everyone got ready to leave, Dawson read the amazing letter from Mike Bick again.

Then he looked at the petition. Carefully.

Where he saw the most amazing thing of all. The very last name on the petition.

Joey Potter.

And following that, a short note from Joey, written so small as to make it difficult to read. It said:

Dawson Leery is the most talented filmmaker any of us is likely ever to meet.

With a lump in his throat, Dawson folded the letter and petition and stuffed them back inside the envelope.

But he didn't put the envelope in his pants pocket.

Instead, with a smile on his face, he put it in the pocket where it really belonged.

Over his heart.